HAGWITCH

Marie-Louise Fitzpatrick

Orion
Children's Books

First published in Great Britain in 2013
by Orion Children's Books
a division of the Orion Publishing Group Ltd
Orion House
5 Upper St Martin's Lane
London WC2H 9EA
A Hachette UK Company

3 5 7 9 10 8 6 4 2

A catalogue record for this book is
available from the British Library.

ISBN 978 1 4440 0637 7

Typeset by Input Data Services Ltd, Bridgwater, Somerset

Printed and bound by
CPI Group (UK) Ltd, Croydon, CR0 4YY

The Orion Publishing Group's policy is to use papers that are
natural, renewable and recyclable products made from wood grown in
sustainable forests. The logging and manufacturing processes are expected to
conform to the environmental regulations of the country of origin.

www.orionbooks.co.uk

For Sarah (Fitzy) – it's been fun for me,
hope it's been fun for you!
And for Niamh White,
who Lally resembles, at least a little bit.
With love, M-L

· ONE

F og creeps. Or so they say. Not this fog. It rose up off the canal water beneath the barge and swallowed it whole. Lally felt the drop in temperature and opened her eyes. Thick murky greyness surrounded the boat. The canal banks, which she knew were close by on either side, had disappeared completely.

She'd been sprawled on the roof for the past hour enjoying some late April sunshine. Now she sat upright and twisted around to squint back towards the stern. Her dad was there guiding the tiller but she couldn't see him. She could hear the familiar chug of the *Beetle*'s engine and the slap of water against the boat's sides but she felt suddenly alone.

She could call out, wait for a reassuring reply.

Don't be daft, she told herself. It's just a bit of weather. Are you a proper water rat or what, Lally McBride?

Water rats – that's what land folk called canal folk. Lally must have been ten or eleven before she'd realised that most people thought those who chose to live on boats were hippy oddballs at best, shifty wasters at worst.

1

Well, even a water rat couldn't see its way through this fog, Lally thought. Easy does it.

She stood up and began to walk along the roof's wet surface towards the barge's back end, moving cautiously. Just as well too. A long screechy noise came from somewhere below the waterline and the *Beetle* shifted abruptly sideways, then stopped with a shudder.

'Ara, blast!' A voice exploded through the fog and the engines cut.

'What have we hit, Eoin?' Lally called.

'Who knows?' Eoin sounded exasperated. Over the last two days they'd had to stop five times to pull the *Beetle* off stuff.

Eoin was Lally's dad but she never called him that. Well, maybe when she was very little, but if she had she didn't remember. She could make out his tall form through the murk now. She stepped down onto the gunnels and manoeuvred along the *Beetle*'s side, swinging around to join him at the tiller. He was staring gloomily over the stern into the water below.

'City canal is a dump.' He scowled. 'It's probably a recently deceased bicycle or a lonely shopping trolley.'

'About time we stopped anyway.' A muffled voice came from below. 'We can't travel in this.'

Des appeared in the doorway. He was only ten years older than Eoin but his manner and the lines on his weather-beaten face meant they were often taken for father and son. They'd known one another forever and had bought the *Beetle* together before Lally was

2

even born. They had taken the old coal barge and transformed it into a small floating theatre, a theatre for puppets. Eoin was the acknowledged puppet expert but he usually deferred to Des on all things barge.

'Whatever we've hit, by the sound of it it gave *Beetle* a mighty scrape before stopping her dead,' Des said, sliding a long pole hook off the roof. 'Hopefully it hasn't damaged the propeller.'

He lowered the pole over the stern and prodded the water with it. 'There. A fallen tree, I'd say.' He pushed down hard. 'No movement. We're lodged fast.'

Eoin crouched, peering into the canal and making sweeping movements with his hands, as if he could swipe the fog away. 'May as well be looking into a bush, as the fella says.'

'Give us a hand then,' Des said.

Eoin stood. He was a good head taller than Des, so he grabbed the pole higher up and the men threw their combined weight onto it, pressing down first onto the canal bed, then onto the thing on which the *Beetle* had gone aground. When that didn't work they aimed the pole at where they knew the left bank should be, found purchase and shoved against it, grunting with the effort.

'Bah!' Des shook his head and stepped back, leaving the pole to Eoin. 'Whatever we're stuck on is dug into the canal bed and *Beetle* is sitting tight on top. There's only one way to get us off it now.'

Eoin groaned and Lally laughed. They both knew what Des meant.

'Time to get the waterproofs on and go in?' Lally suggested.

'Aye. Nothing else for it.' Des grinned at Lally and opened the door to the stairs.

'Your favourite thing of all, Eoin!' Lally giggled, knowing full well her dad would do anything to avoid wading about in the canal. No matter how much waterproof stuff he put on, Eoin would end up covered in mud and wet through. Des would come out of his waders clean as a whistle.

'Well, I could always send you in instead,' Eoin retorted. 'What's the use of having children if you can't exploit them? That's what I say.'

Lally stuck out her tongue in answer to this old joke. 'I'll bet I could get us off that tree in no time,' she said.

'Be my guest, smarty,' Eoin replied as he disappeared below after Des.

I'll bet I could and all, Lally thought. It'd be worth getting a bit wet just to see Eoin and Des's faces.

She tucked a curl behind her ear and grabbed the old broom that was always stowed on the roof. She knelt close to the tiller and gripped it near the base with her left hand. With her head and upper body leaning out over the water, she dipped the broom into the canal and pushed it down until her right arm was in the water up to her elbow.

Whargh! Cold!

Just a tiny bit deeper and she could do it ...

She wedged her feet against a bollard to secure herself

and lowered her arm further into the water. She was in a ridiculously awkward position now, more of her hanging over the stern than was on deck. Her nose was too close to the canal surface for comfort so she twisted her face up to the sky – not that she could see the sky in this fog. Prodding around, she found the space beneath the hull and turned the broom head into it.

There!

In the water the broom bumped alongside something that was not the *Beetle* – a tree, presumably.

Come on, she told herself, gasping at the iciness of the water. Any minute now.

She jiggled the broom about till she felt its head hook securely on what must be a tangle of branches. That would do nicely.

Gotcha, Tree! Ready or not, you and *Beetle* are parting company.

Frowning with the effort of holding the broom at such an uncomfortable angle, she counted to three, then gave one gentle exploratory pull.

The water seemed to tug back against her fingers.

Try again.

This time she'd swear the tree moved slightly towards her before she felt another brief answering pull. As if something down there was dragging on the broom.

Weird.

She twisted her head back towards the water. That's when she saw the face. A woman's face, green and lovely, floating in the canal.

It stared up at Lally with black, cold, curious eyes, its hair floating about its head and twining through what looked like the twisty branches of a drowned tree.

Lally's breath caught hard in her chest. Everything went still and silent, as if the whole world had fallen away from her and there was nothing left. Nothing but her and the strange woman and the surface of the water between them.

The woman was watching her, lips moving as if she was singing, and the eyes ... those eyes ... they were calling Lally in.

Lally's body hardly seemed connected to her brain any more. Without breath or blink she let her face break through the surface of the water. She felt her hair float out around her, mirroring the woman's, as she allowed herself to be pulled towards those dark eyes. She was dimly aware of her feet unhooking themselves from their anchor on the deck and the fingers of her left hand loosening their grip on the tiller.

'Lally?' Eoin's voice above her made her jump. She jerked her head from the water; it rippled and the face dissolved.

'Lal?'

She tightened her hold on the tiller again and turned around to see Eoin and Des watching her, both kitted out in their pull-ups.

She looked back into the water. There *was* a face floating there, watching her. Her own face, watery-green and fixed in a stupefied gawk.

She blinked at her reflection through the hanks of her hair.

This stupid fog has me imagining things.

'What ya doing there, Lally? Are you thinking of going for a swim or just tickling *Beetle*'s belly?' Eoin's eyes were crinkled at the edges, laughing and frowning at the same time. 'Whatever you were up to, I'd rather you'd waited till we were back up on deck to help.'

'Help me now,' Lally said. 'Hang onto me and I'll tickle *Beetle*'s belly, as you call it, one more time.'

Eoin raised his eyebrows but grabbed Lally around the waist as she lowered herself towards the water. She pressed her lips together, tightened her grip on the broom handle and gave it a determined backwards heave. She felt the tree dislodge itself.

'See?' she said, as it came slithering along the underside of the barge. 'You were trying to push and shove us off the tree when it was the tree that needed moving out from under *us*.'

'What? I don't believe you!' Eoin stared over the stern. A slimy black tree trunk bobbed to the surface and the *Beetle* began to shift.

Beside them Des shook his head. 'That doesn't make any sense at all. We were stuck fast on it, I'd swear,' he said. 'But, hey, I won't argue with you; we're off! And this fog is starting to lift. About time. I'll get the engine going. If we don't get a move on it'll be dark by the time we make Old Forge Lock.'

'Hold on,' Eoin said. 'Waste not, want not. That's

a fine big lump of wood; it'll do nicely for the stove. We've got the waders on anyway, may as well use them.'

'It'll be rotten through,' Des protested. 'Probably been in the water for years, it'll be no good to burn.'

'Ah, come on. The canal's not deep here and we won't actually have to go in to get it. Sure, it'll only take us a minute.' Eoin already had the pole hook back in his hand.

'OK, OK,' Des said. 'You work from the bank, I'll work from the deck. No point in both of us falling in.' Des flashed his gap-toothed grin at Lally and rolled his eyes.

She smiled, though she didn't feel much like it. She knew she'd imagined the woman in the water; she must have. Too much sun, too much fog, her eyes playing tricks, whatever, but she was feeling pretty freaked out all the same.

And even from here she could see that the tree was just a lump of trunk. There were no branches on it anywhere. Not a single one.

TWO

Des was right; it was dark by the time they passed through Old Forge Lock. Lally could see the *Ladybird* was already moored up ahead, light glowing through her windows. This smaller barge was home to Carla and Nette, the rest of Lally's theatre family. They'd have arrived at the Old Forge hours ago, having taken the Hertford Union Canal route from the Lee Navigation. The *Beetle* had taken a circuitous route, going down to Bow and across the Limehouse Cut to call at a boat yard and get a small part replaced in *Beetle*'s engine.

Carla stepped off *Ladybird* and walked alongside to help them tie up.

'You lot are very late,' she remarked as she caught *Beetle*'s bow line. 'Was there a big queue at the boat yard?'

'No, no. There was nothing ahead of us and the lad got the job done in record time,' Des answered as he tied up the stern. 'But we hit a thick patch of fog after leaving the Limehouse Basin and himself ran us aground on a tree trunk for good measure.'

'Fog?' Carla raised her eyebrows. 'Sun's been beaming all day here.'

'Must have rolled in from the Thames. We were near the river when it caught us,' Des said. He paused and sniffed the air. 'Something smells good.'

'That'll be Nette's chicken and mushroom pie. It's just out of the oven,' Carla said. 'Ladies' Night tonight, Lally. Some quality girl-time before the craziness of the big city gets us all of a dither. You ready to come over right away?'

Lally nodded. She'd dried herself off after her half-dip in the canal and she was starving.

'Are you and Eoin off to Madigan's for your usual pre-London beer 'n' steak evening?' Carla asked Des.

'As soon as Eoin gets himself cleaned up from his latest dunk in the canal.' Des laughed. 'Fell in pulling this rotten old thing out for firewood.' He kicked at the tree trunk which had been stored with the rest of the woodpile to one side of the door. 'There'll be hardly any burning in it. But you know Eoin.'

'I do.' Carla smiled.

'Get Lal to tell you how she got us unstuck,' Des said as Lally stepped from the *Beetle* to the *Ladybird*. 'Not sure how she did it, but she did.'

Ladybird was totally different to the *Beetle*. Where *Beetle* had a tiller and was steered from outside in all weathers, *Bird* had a wheelhouse. Where *Beetle* had portholes, *Bird* had windows. Carla and Nette's barge was a little floating house, all cosy curtains and cushions, woollen rugs and photographs. *Bird* smelled good too – of baking and herbs and coffee and verbena soap. *Beetle* reeked of diesel and old leather.

The *Beetle* was much larger and older than the *Bird*; a working boat, hulking and functional, the bulk of her taken up by the puppet theatre, and every nook and cranny used for storage. For Lally, both boats were home. Her cabin was in the bows of the *Beetle* but she often slept over on the *Bird*.

Well, she used to. Now that she thought about it, she hadn't slept on *Bird* for at least a year.

Nette waved two bottles in the air as Lally and Carla came through the door. 'Lemonade or ginger beer?'

'Lemonade,' Lally said and plomped down on the built-in settle. 'Here's to the summer season,' Carla said, raising her glass to clink Lally's.

'The summer season,' Lally repeated.

'Though I have to admit,' Carla said, brushing her long dark hair out of her face and sitting on the settle beside Lally, 'I like the winter season best. I prefer the country waterways and putting on shows in the small towns. Everything is slower, the way I like it.'

'Still, it's a nice change to tie up in one place and stay put for a whole four months, even if it is London.' Nette paused in her whisking, drew a finger around the bowl and licked it. 'That's the chocolate mousse ready for the fridge. D'you want the whisk, Lally?'

'Yes, please!'

'I mean, I love travelling the canals but it does get tiring after months and months of it,' Nette continued, beginning to spoon great blobs of mousse into pretty glasses. 'Every Monday, clean up, pack up, dismantle the theatre, fold down *Beetle*'s walls, lower her roof, turn her back into a boat again, set off to the next town …'

'Hand out flyers, put up posters, let them know we've arrived,' Lally added, running her finger along the whisk and putting it in her mouth. 'Yum. Set *Beetle* up again, raise the roof, fix the seats back in place, get ourselves ready for the weekend shows.'

'It has a lovely rhythm to it, though,' Carla said. 'In summer it's show after show after show – matinees, evenings, every day but Monday. I like to move around.' She paused. 'And I suppose I don't really like the city.'

'You can't see it when we're moored in Little Venice,' Lally protested. 'We could be anywhere.'

'Ah, but I know it's out there.' Carla shivered. 'Big bad city stuff, all crowded around us. Hulking great grey buildings, snippy-snappy people rushing about, thousands of cars circling us. Even trains crawling below us, for Pete's sake. No, give me the countryside any day.'

'Don't need to ask which you prefer, Lal.' Nette laughed. 'You're a summer-seasoner, like me.'

Lally shrugged. 'I like them both,' she said.

'Oh, come on!' Nette paused, spoon midway between bowl and glass. 'You've always loved the summer season because of the trainees.'

Lally gathered another fingerful of froth off the whisk and nodded half-heartedly.

The trainees.

Every year during summer season two or three people joined the barge to train in the art of puppeteering. They were young and eager, at different levels of skill and experience, from raw beginners to semi-professional operators, often coming from as far away as Poland, Hungary or France. When Lally was little, this had been the highlight of her year. She was fascinated by these visitors, with their exotic accents and stories of foreign places, and she would spend as much time with them as she could. They were always so sweet to her, treating her like a little sister or a mascot or something. Nette was right; summer was Lally's favourite time of the year.

Was.

Last year she had found herself suddenly overcome with shyness when the two trainees – a boy and a girl – first arrived. She'd got over that eventually, but the girl trainee hadn't been terribly friendly anyway. She'd made it obvious that she thought Lally was just a kid and shouldn't hang around her and the other trainee all the time.

'Though that Anna last year was a bit of a cow,' Nette said, as if she'd read Lally's thoughts. She took a tray of roast potatoes out of the oven and placed it on the table. 'OK. Dinner's up.'

Carla uncurled from the settle and crossed to *Bird*'s

small table. 'I think Markus was your special friend last summer, Lally,' she said as she slid onto the bench fixed to the wooden wall. 'Am I right?'

Lally nodded and concentrated on squeezing into the seat beside her.

Markus, from Germany, *had* been really nice to Lally. He had spent ages talking to her and teaching her chords on his guitar. Then, halfway through the second month of the summer season, Anna, the other trainee, had taken Lally aside and told her that she was annoying Markus and he was just too nice to tell her.

'He needs a bit of space, you know?'the Italian girl had said. 'And you need some friends your own age, darling.'

Lally could feel her skin growing hot just remembering.

'How much pie?' Carla was asking, knife poised over the golden crust. 'It's your favourite. A big piece?'

'Mmm, please,' Lally said, smiling brightly. 'It's warm in here. Shall I open a window?'

She needed to turn away for just a moment. Because now she had started remembering last summer she couldn't stop herself remembering what had happened next. She twisted around and slid the window open. Cool air hit her cheeks.

Two days after her conversation with Anna, Lally had walked in on the girl kissing Markus behind the stage.

It wasn't as if she'd never seen people kissing

14

before. But this had been different somehow. She'd felt embarrassed – when there was no reason why she should be – and angry at Markus, which didn't make any sense at all. She'd stammered 'excuse me' and run past them into her cabin. Where she'd burst into tears and cried for at least ten minutes out of pure confusion.

'There you go.' Carla was saying. 'Potatoes? How many?'

She hadn't seen so much of Markus after that, except when they were doing the shows.

'Two,' Lally said, turning back to the table.

And he never did finish teaching her all the chords to 'Wonderwall'.

'How many trainees will there be this year?' Lally asked as she began dissecting her slice of pie.

'There were two but one has cried off at the last minute. Which will leave us short-handed,' Nette said, placing a bowl of salad in the centre of the table and sitting down. She gave Lally a sharp look. 'I can't believe you're only asking about them now; you normally pester us about the trainees for weeks.'

Lally mumbled something incoherent through a mouthful of food.

'She's French. From Paris,' Carla said. 'A woman who has always wanted to be a puppeteer. I think she's about forty-five.'

'Forty-five?' The trainees were usually students, aged between eighteen and twenty.

'Yeah. Ancient, like us!' Carla teased. Carla was fifty

15

and Nette was forty-six. 'Are you very disappointed?' She and Nette looked at Lally a little anxiously.

'Forty-five?' Lally repeated. 'We've never had a trainee that old before.'

'First time for everything,' Nette said. 'Doesn't matter what age they are or where they're from—'

'—they're all themselves, all different, all the same,' Lally chimed in. 'You say that every year.'

Nette and Carla laughed.

Lally fiddled with her hair. 'I wish she didn't have to come,' she said. 'I wish it could be just us this summer. It's like you always say, Carla – trainees are more hassle than they're worth.'

Carla nodded and Nette glared at her before turning back to Lally.

'Lavender Hale-Bopp McBride!' she said. 'Have you turned into a grumpy teenager when I wasn't looking? Since when do you worry about things being a *hassle*? Sure, we'd never do anything at all if we were afraid of a bit of hassle.' Nette – short for Antoinette – was Irish like Eoin and Des. Her accent always became stronger when she was taken by surprise.

Lally sighed. 'It's just that by the time we get to know them and they get used to the way we do things, it's time for them to leave.'

'But they've become friends.' Nette waved her fork in the air.

'There's no point to it, though, is there?' Lally said. 'They leave. They never come back.'

'Sometimes they do.'

'To visit. And then they go away again.'

She leaned across the table to look at the line of framed photos attached to the sloping walls. Photos from all the summer seasons. Her and Eoin and Carla and Nette and Des with each year's trainees.

I remember most of the names, Lally thought.

But would she remember them if there were no photos and if Carla and Nette hadn't always done a sing-song recitation of the names whenever they looked at the pictures together? She wasn't sure she remembered being that little five-year-old girl in the Aran sweater. The image was so familiar, but only from this side of the glass. Though she did think she recalled the red wool itching her throat.

I look cute, she thought. A big smile and a mop of curls in hippy-dippy hand-made clothes. I look cute and happy. In all the photos. Until last year. Last year I looked like an anxious goose. Last year everything changed.

Why? she wondered. Because I'm older now, not a little girl? When did being happy become difficult?

Eoin's girlfriends were in the photos too. Red-haired Laura smiled out from three of them. Lally had liked Laura.

'Why did Laura leave?' she asked.

Nette shrugged. 'Got sick of the lifestyle; gave up trying to tie Eoin down.' She and Carla exchanged a look then smiled into their wine glasses.

Eoin's girlfriends always left. How many were there? One, two, three, four different women in the photos. Lally's mum was in the very first one.

Mum.

Funny. She'd always called Eoin by his first name, yet she called the woman in this photo 'Mum' even though she'd never known her.

It didn't mean anything. It was just a name, like Fran or Jane. Nette said 'Mum' was just a label and meant nothing if that person didn't do their job. And Lally's mum hadn't done her job. She'd left, when Lally was only a year old. She was no one but a face in a photograph. All she'd given Lally were two crazy names. Lavender – which was too icky for daily use – and Hale-Bopp, after a comet which had been in the sky when Lally was born thirteen years ago.

'Did Eoin love my mum?' Lally asked, tracing a finger over her mother's face.

'What? Of course,' Nette said. 'You're in a funny mood tonight. Everything OK?' She put her knife and fork down on the table.

There was silence for a moment.

'You know you can always ask us anything, Lal? Tell us anything?' Carla said softly.

'Yeah, I know,' Lally said. But she wasn't so sure of that. She'd just asked them a question and 'of course' didn't seem like much of an answer. Now that she tore her eyes away from the photos she could see both Nette and Carla looked halfway between upset and alarmed.

She glanced from one to the other. *They* were her real mums. On the walls there were photos of them holding her as a baby, helping her to walk, playing with her in the little pen they used to keep on deck, so she wouldn't fall overboard.

They were her teachers too. The *Ladybird* was Lally's schoolroom. Carla had taught her to read, write and draw and now she did English literature with her as well as history and art; Nette covered maths and science, geography and cooking.

You've upset them. Change the subject.

'Can I stay the night?'

'Of course you can.' Carla beamed at her. 'It's been ages since you stayed over.' She reached an arm around Lally and pulled her close. 'We'll hook up the spare bed. Now, tell us how you got the *Beetle* off that old tree trunk this afternoon.'

THREE

The fog was back, swirling about the barges, dank fingers clawing along the flat roof to the place where Lally was dozing. Something was lurking just inside the grey, moving swiftly towards her. Lally went from half-asleep to awake, from lying down to sitting upright. The fog kept coming, enveloping her. The lurking thing was at her feet; she could feel its presence. She kicked out frantically, hitting nothing but air.

She shoved herself backwards, desperately trying to get away from the thing in the fog. One of her hands touched the roof edge and the other reached out into nothingness, sending her tumbling overboard. She hit the water and sank below the surface.

It's safer here, she thought, and dived downwards.

No, no, no!

The strange woman was there, just beneath her. Her hair was drifting around her head, tangling in the twisted branches of the tree.

There's no woman, nitwit, she reminded herself. Calm down. It's just your reflection.

She stared at the face. It was hard to see it properly through all that hair and water. She was about to swim closer to take a better look when she remembered

20

something. Something that made her heart skip.

It can't be my reflection. It can't be. I'm underneath the water.

Lally sat up so quickly her head struck the ceiling with a loud crack. She was definitely awake now. She fell back onto the pillow, confused and stunned. Cartoon stars exploded inside her eyes.

Ow! That hurt.

She squeezed her eyes shut and rubbed her forehead. This was the hazard of sleeping onboard *Bird*. The spare bed was created by lifting the back of the settle outwards and hooking it to the ceiling with chains. She'd loved the novelty of it as a kid. Now, as she felt the bump beginning to rise on her temple, she figured she'd officially outgrown it.

A glance at her watch told her it was five a.m. The stupid patch of fog they'd entered yesterday and that slimy bit of trunk they'd gone aground on had really weirded her out. First she was seeing stuff, now she was having creepy dreams. Her heart was beating like crazy and her skin tingled in a cold sweat. She knew the only way she'd get to sleep again was rolled up in her own duvet back on *Beetle*.

She swung her legs over the edge of the bunk and quietly lowered herself to the floor. It took a few minutes to fold the sheet and duvet and put the bed back into its normal position without making a noise. She crept by Nette and Carla's cabin and through the wheelhouse, up onto the deck. Outside it was still

21

pretty dark and no one was stirring yet, though she could hear the hum of early traffic on nearby roads. As she stepped on board the *Beetle*, she carefully avoided the woodpile and its newest bit of firewood.

Lally loved *Bird* but she loved *Beetle* more – she had been born on board the *Beetle*, after all. And the *Beetle* was a very special boat. Moving through the canals she was just another barge. Moored, she transformed, with half a day's hard work, into a floating theatre. Eoin and Des had designed the ingenious folding panels which gave *Beetle* added height, raising her roof to allow ten rows of red leather seats to tier upwards inside her, facing the little stage. A marionette's stage.

As she expected, the *Beetle*'s door wasn't locked. Lally let herself in and tiptoed down the stairs and through the living area of the barge, which was nicknamed 'the chow house'. As she entered the stage area she saw she was being watched. A small zebra, a horse and a rabbit were sitting solemnly in the front-row seats, their little bead eyes glittering in the dimness. Normally Zee, Hippity and Hoppity hung on the wall, their legs posed to run, but when the *Beetle*'s walls were folded down, like now, the puppets that adorned those walls sat like a miniature audience in the first two rows.

'Sorry,' she whispered. 'Go back to sleep. All of you, go back to sleep.'

In the second row, Cinders, Cat, Old Dog, Hansel and Gretel were all cast in shadow, but Lally knew they were there, watching, listening.

She hadn't talked to them in a long time. When had she stopped talking to the puppets?

It had been part of her bedtime ritual when she was little to walk about the *Beetle* with Eoin, asking all the puppets how their day had been. Eoin would take a different one from the wall each night, working its strings and giving it a voice. When she was old enough to walk down to her cabin alone at night she had continued to chat to each of them, feeling it rude to pass them by without enquiring after their health and wishing them sweet dreams. Somewhere along the way that had become a general goodnight, and then a silent one, said inside her head. Without noticing, some time in the last year, she'd stopped doing that too.

'Goodnight, everyone,' she whispered now.

She passed in front of the stage and walked through the tiny backstage area to her own door. Her cabin took up the port side of the bows, and her bunk was shaped into the curved wall. The street light was still on, streaming through the porthole, throwing shadows around her tiny room. Bear and Wolf stared at her from one wall. Lally had never had dolls; with a barge full of puppets she didn't need them. Bear and Wolf were her favourites and shared her cabin when not being used in a show.

She looked around the room with its stick-on glitter butterflies and frilly pink curtains.

This is a little girl's room, she thought. What age

was I when Carla helped me put all this pink stuff up? Eight?

She flopped onto her bunk and reached up to the nearest butterfly, picking at a corner with her nails. The wings came away easily, but the body took a bit of effort. It left an empty butterfly shape in the paintwork. She started on another. If she picked a couple off every time she was in the room she'd have them all off in a few days. And those curtains had to go.

There is a hessian sack in the galley. I bet it'd make a cool blind, she thought. And if Bear and Wolf weren't here I could stick up a poster or something.

The puppets' eyes reproached her from their brown wooden faces.

'You'll be needed on-stage in a couple of days anyway,' she said to them, apologetically. 'You're in the summer play.'

She tossed the bits of butterfly in the bin, pulled the frilly curtains over the porthole one last time, turned away from Bear and Wolf and closed her eyes.

29th day of April, in the year of our Lord 1596

I spot them approaching as I sit at my desk in the open upstairs window. The three men are winding through the crowded lane below me, lugging something large. Well, Nashe and Hobbes are doing the lugging; Bennet, as always, is leading the way, issuing instructions and bidding them to get a move on.

What is it they've got?

My curiousty is roused. Master Waller's back is turned; he is bent over his work in the far corner of the chamber. I stand up quietly, push both windows fully open, and stick my head out to look down onto the street.

Ah, so that's what it is. It must be sore heavy. Hobbes and Nashe have stopped to hoist it onto their shoulders. How funny they look now! Hobbes being so much taller than Nashe and what they carry being so cumbersome, it has them all out of kelter. As they pass beneath the casement their load is almost on level with me; I could reach out and touch it. I almost do. Just in tyme I snatch my hand back. I feel the smile fall from my face.

Zounds! They mustn't bring that in the house!

I throw my quill aside and sprint downstairs fast as I can but they are already within.

'Do not bring that in here, do not let it cross the threshold!' I shout, charging across the hall. 'Take it out, take it out!' I even push Bennet back towards the door in my alarm.

Pushing Bennet isn't a good idea. He stops abruptly. Hobbes walks into him, stumbles and drops his end of the thing, which falls, catching Nashe in knee and foot.

'Ow, ow, ow!' Nashe lets go too and begins to hop around holding his big toe. The tree trunk thunks to the floor and rolls slowly into the centre of the hall, sending up stale stinks and scents as it disturbs the dirt and herbs amongst the rushes.

Bennet arches his eyebrows and a leisurely smile spreads across his handsome face. That's a smile I have learned not to trust, for often as not it ends in a sore ear for me.

'And why, pray thee, should we not bring it in?' His voice is honeyed, as if he's asking his sweetheart for a kiss.

''Tis bad luck, it'll bring calamities on us all!' I stutter.

'Hasn't Master Waller been telling us these last three weeks that he requires a tree trunk to stand centre stage in his new play?'

'But not hawthorne, he never meant for you to bring hawthorne.' I stare in horror at the newly-felled trunk. A cut at one end has severed it cleanly from its roots but the top cut, done to take away the branches, has been ill-done, hacked and jagged and leaving one small forlorn branch attached, with some leaves and a single early flower.

26

'Oak, beech, hawthorne, elder – what's the difference? A tree is a tree. Do not tell me you believe those old wives' tales, Bacon, my boy. I thought we'd knocked the country bumpkin out of you.'

I wince. He hasn't called me Bacon this last month or more.

'You'll always be Bacon to us.' That's what he told me when I first arrived in London three months back. ''Tis what us town folk call you country folk. Look at you! All pink-faced and rosy! There may not be much pork on you, but a Bacon you are all the same.'

I thought it would only make matters worse when my sister Mary called by early in March with a parcel of pork tripe sausages my mother had sent for me, but Bennet had taken quite a fancy to Mary. He'd been fair tickled when he'd heard her call me by my family pet name.

'Flea?' Bennet had roared with laughter. 'Flea? You call him Flea? And well it suits him too! There's not much of him and he jumps a mile at the slightest thing!'

From then on the company all called me Flea and I was Bacon no more.

Until now.

'Do tell us what the old dames say of hawthorne, Bacon,' Bennet says, his eyes glittering in the gloom of the hall. 'Go on, amuse me. You know how I love to be amused.'

Nashe is sitting on the floor, his foot twisted up almost to his nose as he inspects it for damage, and Hobbes has collapsed on a stool, mopping his massive brow with a filthy handkerchief, but they look up, grinning, to see what sport Bennet means to have with me. Tom appears from the kitchen, scratching his face. He is the nearest thing I have to a friend in this house but that's only when the others aren't about. I know that if they choose to make a fool of me now he will laugh when they do, and twice as heartily.

'What's going on?' he asks, drawing blood from one of the many pimples on his cheek.

'Yes, what is going on?' a mild voice asks from above our heads.

We look up at the balcony. Our employer, Master Waller, has appeared out of the work chamber, quill in hand. 'What sent you tearing off in such a hurry, Flea? Why this noise and disturbance?'

'We found you a tree trunk, Master Waller,' Nashe announces. 'Already felled, and abandoned in the middle of the road. We just trimmed off the top branches, is all.'

'Stand aside, let me see.' Master Waller peers down and Bennet sweeps an elaborate bow, indicating the lump of wood with the feather on his hat. 'Yes, yes, that will do nicely. Dark wood, twisted, somewhat gnarled – it has character. Well done. Well done.'

'But Bacon here claims it's bad luck and we must toss it out, sir,' Bennet says slyly. He grabs my hand and pulls me into view.

'Bacon? O, you mean Flea. What possible objection can you have to the tree trunk, boy?' Master Waller turns to me and blinks.

28

I think to tell him about the time a single hawthorne petal curdled a whole pail of cow's milk on my mother or of the story my granddam told me of a maid who once brought a bouquet of the flowers indoors and how, within a year, her family were all taken by the pox. But Bennet's watching me, his left eyebrow raised up and his lip curling. Hobbes and Nashe are elbowing each other and sniggering. Worst of all I think I see disappointment in Master Waller's pale blue eyes.

'It's … it's a hawthorne tree, Master Waller,' is all I say.

'And?'

'My mother taught me never to bring so much as a branch of it into the house, Master Waller,' I reply, as stoutly as I can under all their scornful stares. 'And now here is a whole trunk, freshly felled. It will bring bad luck, sir.'

'Bad luck?'

'It's sacred to the faery folk. So my mother says.' My voice falters and this last comes out a whisper. I hear the others choking and spluttering as they hold in their laughter. My face begins to burn.

'I see.' Master Waller frowns and tutts. Just once. Softly. But I've heard it and hang my head. He is my first master, and a good man. I have taken great pains with my work; I wish him to think well of me.

'I know the old tales,' he says, 'but I have no tyme for such peasant nonsense. I thought you a cleverer fellow than – well, no mind to that. I am sorry if its presence here makes you uncomfortable.' He pauses and strokes

29

his pointed beard. 'It is a very fine trunk. Perfect for my needs. Go have a tisane in the kitchen then come back to your desk, Flea. I have almost finished the play at last; you have much copying to do. The rest of you go about your business. Rehearsals will begin the day after tomorrow. There is only one day's leisure left to you, so make the most of it and stop loitering about here.' He makes a shooing gesture at us, turns back into his chamber and closes the door.

I clench my fists and wait for the teasing and the laughter to begin in earnest, but Bennet and the other actors are all too excited by our employer's last words to bother with what has gone before.

'It's nearly done?' Hobbes booms, a happy smile breaking across his face. 'The new play is ready?'

'About tyme,' says Bennet. 'I'm rested quite enough, thank you. Ready to tread the boards again.' He catches Tom to him in a mock embrace and dances him lightly around the hall. 'Are you ready to be romanced, Thomasina?' he cackles, lifting Tom easily into the air and depositing him on the other side of the killed tree.

Tom flutters his eyelids and drops a curtsey. 'I am, fine sir,' he says, raising his voice a little to that of a maiden's sing-song. 'Though my mother may not approve if I give my heart to a vagabond actor the likes of you.'

'Ah, but I'm to be a duke this tyme.' Bennet strikes a pose, hand on hip and handkerchief at nose. 'Your mama can have no objection to a duke, surely?'

Tom clasps his hands across his chest and feigns girlish

delight. I try to imagine him as he would be on stage, dressed as a lass with periwig, make-up and gown. From where I'm standing he looks like any young lad, same age as me, only with very bad skin.

'Tyme for a celebration ale, my friends,' Bennet says, rubbing his hands together. 'Where shall we grace with our custom this merry afternoon? The George or the White Hart?'

He leads them out the door, all chatter and laughter. I am left, forgot, standing here with the wretched tree trunk, and it bleeding green sap all over the stone flags.

FOUR

'Lights on below?' Eoin asked, as Lally stepped on deck with an armful of torches.

'Lights on,' she said, pulling her hood up against the driving rain.

'Distribute the torches, First Mate, we're going in,' Eoin said, his face deep inside the hood of his rain jacket.

Lally clambered onto the roof and placed the red torch to port and the green to starboard, switching them on as she went. Over on *Ladybird*'s deck, Des and Carla were doing the same thing, part of the preparation ritual for entering the Islington Tunnel. The tunnel was a half mile of darkness so the barges always went in lit up as much as possible.

'Torches on?' Eoin had to raise his voice to be heard above the rain.

'Torches on, Captain!' Lally called back, flashing the one in her hand on and off and taking her position at the bow. On *Bird*'s bow, Des gave an answering flicker and Nette waved from the wheelhouse.

'Engage engines!' Eoin shouted, turning the *Beetle*'s key. 'Here's hoping nothing comes the other way while we're in there!'

The *Beetle* thrummed into life. Narrowboats could pass each other in the tunnel but barges like *Beetle* and *Bird* took up most of its width.

'Might be drier in there than out here, at any rate,' he said. 'The ghosts of the Islington Tunnel, make way for the *Beetle* and *Ladybird!*'

'That's my signal.' Carla laughed and jumped onto the bank. 'See you at the other end.'

They all waved. Carla had announced this morning that now Lally was old enough to help navigate the tunnel she would not be putting herself through the torture of being inside it.

'But it's fun, you've always said so.' Lally had been surprised, thinking of all the years Carla had wrapped her arms around her as they'd entered the tunnel, held her and told her not to be afraid.

'I don't know which of us I was trying to convince, love. That's one long tunnel; it always creeps me out. The dark, the weight of the city on our heads … Well, not this time. I'll follow the trail of waymarkers up here in the open air and meet you at the west portal.'

The east portal squatted dank and black ahead. Lally felt a slight quiver in her stomach but nothing like the almost hysterical anticipation she'd have felt when she was little. Then, she'd have started counting the bridges as soon as they left the Hertford Union. By the time they passed under the one at Frog Lane she'd have been fairly jumping up and down. It was excitement and fear all mixed together and she'd shiver and giggle and shriek inside Carla's arms as the *Beetle* entered the east portal.

'All clear?' Eoin called from the tiller.

Lally peered ahead. It was dark inside. She couldn't see any barge lights. In this grey weather she couldn't even see the tiny pinprick of light at the other end of the tunnel. She signalled a thumbs-up. Eoin flicked on the headlights and sounded the horn. As the bow entered Lally heard a soft thunk and shuffle behind her. A bird had chosen this moment to land on the roof looking for crumbs.

'Shoo!' She waved her free hand at it. 'Shoo, you stupid thing.'

'Kak!' it replied. 'Kak, kak.' It blinked its blue eyes but it didn't move.

'Shoo! SHOO! Eoin, we're bringing a jackdaw in with us.' She half stood and waved to catch his attention.

'Too late now.' He shrugged. 'Keep your head down and your eyes ahead. Want to sing the tunnel song? *Islington Tunnel is long and dark—*' he began.

'*Once you're in you can't go back,*' Lally continued. '*With a hey and a ho and give the dog a shoe,* the Beetle *barge is coming through.*'

Her voice rolled around the walls, echoing away from her. That had been part of the thrill of the tunnel, she and Carla making silly noises and waiting for them to fall away into silence. If you shrieked, squawked, helloed and yahooed in quick succession you could fill the tunnel with a whole village of voices and frighten yourself half-silly in the process.

'Kak,' said the jackdaw.

'Kak yourself,' Lally said. She was sure she should have felt honoured to have the company of a wild bird through the tunnel but actually the thing scared her a little. She swung the full glare of the torch on it.

'Sssshhhh!' It jumped towards her and clicked its beak.

'Hey, Lally!' Eoin called. 'Keep that torch pointed forwards please. Eyes on the water. Anything there?'

'Umm, I'm looking.' Lally reluctantly turned her back on the bird and did a quick survey. 'The odd plastic bottle and some beer cans. Nothing the *Beetle* can't handle.'

It really was dark in here; *Beetle*'s headlights and the torches barely dinted the blackness. Lally found herself curling inwards, tucking her legs tight, squeezing her arms around her knees, ducking her head. The walls of the tunnel were close on either side, close enough to reach out and drag her fingers along, if she felt so inclined.

She didn't.

In the torchlight the walls looked slimy; years of city grease, coal dust and diesel fumes had caked the old bricks. She glanced at the jackdaw. It was hunched down with its beak tucked into its breast. Probably as scared of her as she was of it.

'I hope we don't get stuck,' she whispered to it. 'I

hope the engine doesn't break down.'

The bird scampered backwards a few steps.

'We're more than halfway in now. Next stop, Camden Town,' she said. 'You can fly away home.'

They'd moor in Camden for lunch and to take on supplies, like always. After that the canal would take them into Regent's Park, through the tiny Eyre's Tunnel and the one at Maida Hill. Then they'd be at their summer moorings – Little Venice.

'Why don't I feel excited about things any more, Mister Jackdaw?' she whispered. 'Why am I dreading it this time? What's changed? Is it me?'

Forty-five. This year's trainee was forty-five. She'd arrive tomorrow, dragging way too much luggage and wearing the wrong shoes.

'Would I prefer it if she was eighteen?' Lally whispered to the jackdaw.

What difference did it make? Whatever age the trainees were, they were never the same age as Lally. No matter how friendly any of them were, she was just a little kid to them.

'Shall I tell you something pathetic, Jackdaw?' she said. 'I have no friends. Little Lally-no-mates, that's me. We never stay anywhere long enough, that's the problem. When we travel in the country we only stay a week in any town.'

And in London there were never kids around outside of show times.

Except one year. Lillian and Rosemary year.

'When I was nine there were two girls called Lillian and Rosemary staying with their grandparents on one of the narrowboats in Little Venice,' Lally whispered to the bird. 'They were both younger than me, but I didn't care. We played together all summer. It was great. But then their grandfather died and their gran sold the boat so they never came again.'

'Kak,' said the bird.

'Pitiful, eh? Told you so.' Lally bit her lip. 'But just once, Jackdaw. Just once, I'd like someone my age to hang out with.'

'Kak.' The bird suddenly sounded close by. She twisted her head. It was hunched less than a metre away, its gaze flicking from her to the growing ball of light at the end of the tunnel.

'Nearly there,' she called to Eoin.

'*Islington Tunnel is dark and long,*' he sang.

'*To pass the time we sing this song, with a hey and a ho, give the dog a crown, here we come Old Camden Town.*'

There was a sound of scuffling from behind and a whirr of wings. Lally ducked instinctively just as the jackdaw skimmed close over her head.

'Ka-aak,' it said.

She watched as it flew away from her and the *Beetle*, disappearing through the curtain of rain at the west portal.

The 30th day of April, 1596

*M*aster *Waller's* tearing pages. I can hear him moaning and flinging himself about the work chamber, ripping sheets as I come up the stairs. I gingerly open the door. There's paper everywhere – on the floor, on the desks, in mid-air. I know what this means. What was near finished yesterday is considered not good enough today. He has destroyed it all.

'I must begin anew, Flea,' Master Waller says despondently. 'Clean it away please, so I may start again. Then leave me. I'll have no need of you today.'

His hands are shaking. They are long and thin. The skin is pale, almost blue-tinged, fingernails neat and clean. How does he write all day long and hardly get one blot of ink on them? My own fingers are permanently black, my ragged nails ringed all about with the stain of gall.

'What's the use?' He's talking to himself so I avert my eyes and begin to gather up the wasted paper, the wasted words. 'Why do you persist?' he mutters. 'You are a fool, a pitiful, abject failure!' He almost sobs. He catches one knuckle between his teeth and stops himself.

38

I kneel on the floor and gather torn sheets of play into my arms. His flowing hand is on some fragments, my neat, careful copyings on others. Master Waller flops in his chair and watches me pick up the pieces. From what little I know of him he is normally a temperate man. He eats and drinks moderately. He keeps regular hours, he attends church. He rarely raises his voice; his movements are elegant and measured. Yet this is the third tyme since I have come to work as his scrivener that he has taken his work and torn it asunder. Three times, in so many months! The actors will be upset when they hear it.

He is in control again, breathing deeply. The act of destruction seems to have calmed him. I'm still wondering how badly Bennet and the other actors will take this latest delay when I find myself backing into something. I turn and see the tree trunk.

God's bread! I've touched it!

I had noticed it was gone from the hall as soon as I got up. I'd hoped someone had taken it away, at least put it out of the house, if not taken it back to where it was found. Now here it is, standing on its end, in my master's work chamber.

'It will make a fine stool, I think,' Master Waller says vaguely in my direction. 'Once the top end has been filed down and smoothed.'

He pulls his chair back to his desk. It's a perfectly sound chair of good design and fine workmanship. Anyone would be proud to have such a piece within their household. Why on Earth would he replace it with a rough tree trunk? I almost speak my thoughts aloud but Master Waller has begun scratching at a fresh page with his goose quill and indicates the door with his other hand.

'The man's a talentless fool,' Bennet fumes when I pass on the news to him and the others in the yard of the George Inn. 'A self-deluding, self-indulgent talentless fool!'

Hobbes stares gloomily into his ale tankard. 'I suppose we should be grateful for the roof over our heads and a week's wages for doing nowt.'

'But how long's his money going to last?' Nashe flops his head down onto his folded arms. 'How many months is it since the last play? How many weeks since we last proclaimed his convoluted sentences in public and got pelted by market rubbish for our troubles?'

'Bah! If this play is as bad as the last we'll be lucky to escape the stage with our lives,' Hobbes exclaims through a mouthful of lark and pigeon pie.

'But Master Waller writes so well!' I protest, brushing pastry crumbs off my jerkin.

'Ah! You're an expert in the art of the playwright, are you?' Bennet asks. 'Pray, tell me, Bacon, how many plays have you attended in your short and miserable life?'

'N-none,' I admit. 'But yesterday I copied full twenty-two times the word 'perchance'. And many times 'wherewithal' and 'forsooth'. And lots of other large words I do not know the meaning of, besides.'

'But what's the play about? Can you tell me that?'

I fall silent. I must confess the plot has me confused. Each character seems much like the other.

'You only have to transcribe his words, Flea,' Tom says sourly. 'You do not have to speak them to a thousand people.'

'When did we ever perform one of Waller's plays to a thousand people?' Bennet snorts. 'His name doesn't draw the crowds. He's not a playwright of genius like Marlowe, nor even a decent wit like Lyly.' Bennet twists the earring in his left ear so violently I expect blood. 'Ours is not the usual acting life, Flea. Waller keeps us, houses us, pays us wages, we are Waller's Men, but he does not live off the wages of his words. If he did, he'd starve and us along with him. A real playwright has to write better and faster than he, maybe creating as many as four plays a year. If we were a normal company of actors we would be performing Waller's works, new and old, two days every other week, and someone else's plays between times. But he rarely finishes anything he starts and there's no demand for what he has written; no play of his has ever made more than two days' run.' He pulls a face. 'It's been so long since we last trod the boards I fear I have forgot all my skills. This moment I'd happily perform anything! A child's rhyme, an old dame's bequests, a maiden's prayer, even the most pretentious nonsensical twaddle Master Waller can produce – anything to be on stage.'

Bennet jumps to his feet. 'Wherefore,' he intones. 'Whither, whence, hence, dither, thither, fa, fa, fa, fa, fa!' He waves his arms about and rolls his eyes. 'Whenceforth,

henceforth, haffle, paffle, whiffle, sniffle, fi, fi, fi!'

I laugh at his antics with the rest.

'Sit, Flea,' he says, pulling me down on the bench with him. He shoves his empty plancher in front of me, indicating with his hands that I may eat it now he's done with the stew it held. 'Fine words mean nothing if they are strung together with no more wit than so many pretty beads on a thread. There must be meaning, passion, humour. There must be a plot!' He thumps the table and those nearest us turn around and gawp.

'With a beginning, middle and end,' Hobbes adds, picking his teeth with a small bone he has found in his pie.

'There must be a hero—' Bennet's on his feet again, '—brave and true, who encounters many obstacles!'

'A faithful friend,' says Nashe, leaping up likewise, '—who will certainly be horribly wounded, possibly die!'

'And a heroine, lovely and sweet-natured—' Tom gets to his feet, brushes imaginary curls from his face and clutches his hands to his breast, '—in great peril!'

'From an enemy—' Hobbes lurches up, almost upending the table and causing all the tankards to rattle, '—an enemy so vile and fearsome that the audience are moved to hiss whenever he makes an entrance.'

'On guard, Scoundrel!' Bennet draws an imaginary sword and points it at Hobbes, who draws another phantom blade and swirls it in the air.

'Prepare to die, Fool,' roars Hobbes.

Bennet thrusts and Hobbes retreats; Bennet thrusts again, Hobbes parries, then attacks. Bennet dances away across the yard, twisting between the tables and benches, Hobbes crashing after him. Diners all around us grab their planchers and their ales but are amused rather than annoyed. Hobbes rounds a pillar and traps Bennet in a corner.

'Ha! Beg for mercy, ere I slice you in two!' yells Hobbes, throwing his arms upwards in triumph. Bennet dives under one outstretched arm then springs lightly onto the nearest table. Hobbes does a comical double-take, gives an outraged roar, turns and jumps after Bennet, his fleetness of foot surprising me. The table wobbles under both their weight; Bennet jumps from that table to the next, and Hobbes leaps after him. The sword fight continues with much swearing and many near misses. The crowd cheer encouragement for both the hero and his foe; and yet, this play is all for me. The actors begin to fight their way back to where I sit, delivering all their lines and movements to me. I am enthralled.

'There must be blood spilt at the end,' Nashe shouts. 'Swords must clash, the audience must fear the worst!'

'My love, my hero!' Tom cries out to Bennet, then clutches hysterically at those imagined curls and feigns a swoon straight to the ground at my feet.

Above me Bennet and Hobbes both plunge their swords towards each other. They come together in a death embrace, so close we cannot see who has wounded who. Everyone falls silent as both men writhe above us, faces registering shock and pain.

Who shall live, who shall die? I hold my breath.

They break apart. Hobbes coughs, groans, grabs his belly.

'Master Innkeeper,' he splutters. 'Your damned pie has killed me!' And he falls head-first off the table, tumbles and lands flat on the ground beside Tom.

Everyone laughs and claps, and the actors stand and take their bows, still in character. Tom and Bennet hold hands like sweethearts, whyle Hobbes growls and snarls like a villain. When they are all seated again the innkeeper slaps down free ale and scolds Hobbes for maligning his good pies.

Bennet puts tuppence down in front of Tom. 'Take this coney of a lad to the playhouse, for pity's sake. He may be the only one among us who's had schooling, but he has a large gap in his learning all the same.' He slaps me playfully on the shoulder. 'There's a new play by Master Shakespeare at the Curtain this afternoon. Go, Flea! Go see real talent. Go hear the words sing, whisper to your soul. Feel them tickle your ribs, then pierce your very heart.'

FIVE

A mug of hot chocolate, that's what I need, Lally thought, as she hooked up the last light in the backstage area.

It always took hours to get the *Beetle* back into theatre mode. Everyone was needed on deck to get the roof raised and unfold the walls to their full height. When that was done they all had their set jobs; Lally's was sorting out backstage. She climbed down the ladder and walked into the theatre area. The audience benches were all in place, the puppets were up on their hooks. Des and Eoin were nowhere to be seen. In the galley, Lally placed a pan of milk on the hob and stared out of a porthole. It had been late when they'd arrived the evening before and the rain had kept them below deck.

At least it's dry today, she thought. Sun's out and Little Venice is as lovely as ever. It's like being in our own private pond.

Though she did understand what Carla meant about knowing that London was out there. Two days of barging through the city to reach Little Venice from their last stop in the country left no doubt that they were surrounded by millions of people and tons of concrete. The barges had passed through suburb after suburb, a mix of down-at-heel and fixed up, old industrial buildings, flashy new apartment complexes, graffitied council flats, towpaths closed off with barbed wire, and carefully kept bankside with seats and dog-poo bins.

It had been a relief yesterday when the barges had finally emerged from the Maida Hill Tunnel to the last little strip of the Regent's Canal. The lines of pretty painted narrowboats seemed to welcome them. Some barge dwellers had come out to wave hello.

'Summer is coming!' one man had shouted. 'The *Beetle* and *Ladybird* are as good a sign of the season as the swallows, I reckon.'

The area was called Little Venice because of its canals, three of them converging at this point to form a large pool, which even had its own island, Brownings Island, named after the poet Robert Browning. The *Beetle* and *Ladybird* were allowed moorings within the pool itself and from where she stood Lally could see the island, its willows dripping gracefully into the water, touching their own reflections. The city really was nowhere to be seen from this angle because the pool was below street level, enclosed by walls and railings, which in turn were surrounded by fine old trees.

We're here, Lally thought. Summer season is officially beginning. The trainee will be nice. It will be great. Like the summers used to be. Everything's going to be OK, Lally McBride.

Blast! She turned back to the stove in time to see the milk spill over the sides of the pot in an angry sizzle.

And that was the last of the carton. Blast again! *Bird* had all the new supplies. Oh well, Nette made better hot chocolate anyway.

Lally realised she was frowning and forced herself to smile.

Summer will be what I make of it. If I'm determined to enjoy it, it will be good.

She ran up the stairs and out onto the deck.

'All done with the stage, Lal?' Eoin appeared out of *Ladybird* nursing a steaming mug. 'Carla's got a fresh pot of tea down below if you want some.'

'I'm after hot chocolate,' she said. 'Before the trainee arrives.'

'Too late! If I'm not mistaken, this is her coming now.' Eoin looked beyond Lally to where a set of steps came down to the pool from the street above. A woman was struggling on the steps, wrestling a large suitcase. Eoin stepped forward to help.

'Would you be Claudine?' he asked as he grabbed the handle and swung the case down to the flagstones.

The woman blinked her large brown eyes rapidly. 'Yes. That is me. I am Claudine Bertrand.'

A boy appeared behind her on the steps. He looked about Lally's age and his face was set in a serious frown. He flicked Lally a look, then stopped where he was and stared at his feet.

'I am Claudine,' the woman repeated, smiling nervously. 'And this is my son, Gilles.'

SIX

'My ex-husband was supposed to have Gilles for the next four months; it was all arranged. Then suddenly he said he had to go on a business trip and he couldn't take Gilles after all. I – I was afraid if I rang and told you there would be two of us, you would tell us not to come.' Claudine gestured towards the barges. 'If there is no room to have him we will go home, of course. But I am hoping so much ... I thought if we took the chance of arriving...' She trailed off and looked hopefully at Eoin.

Her English was good but her voice went up and down in unexpected places, stretching and pulling some words and shortening others, silencing the last letters of some and landing firmly on others. Lally knew Eoin's frown was only concentration as he took in what she had said, but the stricken look on Claudine's face suggested she feared the worst.

'Well, may we at least see the barge before we leave? It looks so charming.' She stretched her mouth across her face in a resigned grimace and raised her eyebrows and hands in an upwards plea. Lally had never seen anyone shrug with their mouth before.

'Of course you may— What? No, no.' Eoin shook his

head and laughed. 'I mean, you're not going anywhere. We'll squeeze you both in, no problem.'

'Excuse?' Claudine blinked at him, then smiled a huge delighted grin. 'We can stay? Oh, thank you, thank you, thank you! I have been worrying all the way across the Channel Tunnel. Gilles, we can stay.' She turned to her son, who took this news without any change of expression.

'Jill, was it?' Eoin held out a hand to the boy who took it briefly then went back to studying his sneakers.

'Gilles,' corrected Claudine, pronouncing the name like 'eel', with a soft g in front. 'Pronounced 'J-ee-l.'

'Ge-eel,' repeated Eoin. 'Welcome aboard to you both. This is my daughter, Lally. She'll give you the grand tour, won't you, Lal? I've got some errands to run. The rest of the company will be up from their tea break soon.' He tugged at his unruly mop of hair as if he was tipping a cap.

'Claudine will be sleeping in one of the jail cells and Ge-eel can take a hammock,' he said to Lally before patting her encouragingly on the shoulder and heading off down the towpath.

Claudine turned her brilliant smile expectantly to Lally.

'Um, this way,' Lally said, smiling back. 'This is the *Beetle*, also known as the Theatre Barge. Mind your heads – the door is low – and watch your step on the stairs, they're very steep.'

She half-thought the boy wasn't going to follow them but he did, putting down his haversack and taking the suitcase from his mother. He sized up the stairs silently and swung the case in ahead of him. Lally and Claudine reached for it and together lowered it to the ground.

'This is our main living space. We call it the chow house because it's where we eat,' Lally said, indicating the space around them. 'That's the kitchen over there, but we call them galleys on boats.' She pointed to the space which wrapped around the port side of the stairs.

Claudine walked into it, ooh-ing and aah-ing over the neatness of how everything fitted and the cleverness of the storage. She was petite and she moved about the barge easily.

'That's Eoin's cabin.' Lally pointed to the door on the starboard side of the stairs.

She led Claudine over to a door in the wooden wall directly opposite the stairs and the boy followed. 'This is the head – that's what we call the toilet.' She opened the door and stood back. Claudine's smile visibly wobbled as she looked inside the tiny room and Lally thought she saw a flicker of amusement on the boy's face.

He still hadn't said anything, though. Maybe he didn't have much English. And she had about six words of French. Please, please let him speak English.

'That pump is for flushing the head,' she explained, pointing to a black knob located to the left of the toilet.

'You push it up and down to make the water come in and out.'

'Mmm. I see. And where is my "jail cell", as Eoin called it?' That funny mouth shrug again.

'Your cabin is there.' Lally pointed to one of the other doors in the wall.

'Ah! I thought those are, perhaps, cupboards.'

'Well.' Lally opened the door to reveal one of the windowless spaces known to all on the *Beetle* as the cells. 'They kind of are cupboards. The other one belongs to Des.'

'Oh! But there is a bed. And my suitcase will just about fit in. Perfect! Why does the ceiling slope?'

'The cells run underneath the theatre space. The top rows of seating are just above our heads.'

'The theatre! I am dying to see it, aren't you, Gilles?' The boy grunted and instead of following them he picked up his mother's case. As Lally led Claudine down the narrow passageway towards the stage she could hear him manoeuvring it into the cabin.

What age was he? Thirteen like her, she figured.

'Magnifique!' Claudine exclaimed as she stepped into the theatre. The rows of seats were all in place now and the curtains were drawn slightly across the stage. 'Look, Gilles!' she said, as her son walked into the theatre. 'The puppets! The beautiful puppets.'

She went from wall to wall, gently touching Zebra, Hippity, Hoppity and the others, admiring the workmanship and examining the joints.

'Where do I sleep?' Gilles asked suddenly. He looked straight at Lally for the first time. His eyes were big and brown, like his mother's, with the same long dark lashes. Lally wondered if he could do the mouth shrug too. She also wondered what he thought about being dragged from Paris to come and stay on a barge for the summer. Not much, if the look on his face was anything to go by. But at least he spoke English.

'Um, you'll be in a hammock; they're kept in here with the pillows and sleeping bags.' She opened the box in front of the stage. 'You can stow your stuff in here.'

'Where does the hammock hang?' he asked.

'Up there.' Lally pointed to hooks attached to the roof above the seats. 'I've slept in them. They're really comfortable.'

Gilles stared upwards. 'OK,' he said. And there it was; the mouth shrug.

What did it mean? He was happy OK or so-so OK? Lally tried to figure out his expression but he turned away to put his haversack on the storage box.

'And who is this?' Claudine pointed to the faces pressed to one of the starboard portholes. Lally looked up to see Nette and Carla waving in at them.

'That's the rest of the company,' Lally explained. 'Come and meet them.'

On the towpath Lally made introductions and stepped back in relief as the others took over answering Claudine's questions. She found herself standing beside Gilles. She glanced at him but he was staring off into the distance as if he wished he was somewhere else.

Great! she thought. Someone my age finally comes onboard for the summer and it looks like the last place he wants to be is here.

The 2nd day of May, 1596

'*H*ow now, bold Flea?' Tom raises his head from the bowl of gruel he's eating. He eyes the goose feathers in my hand. 'Annie will not let you sharpen those in here.'

'Indeed I will not,' says Annie, without turning from the stirring of her pot. 'Off outside with you both and let me have my kitchen free.'

I follow Tom out the back door and we settle on the steps. I take out my penknife and set to trimming the quills for use.

'I thought Master Waller liked to sharpen his own pens,' remarks Tom, between slurps.

'He does,' I say. 'And usually he uses the same one for days on end. He mends and trims it as he writes. He says it gives him tyme to think. But not today – today he bade me get a half a dozen pens ready and to check the supply of ink as well. Then he ordered me to quit the work chamber, for he says my very breathing is distracting him.'

'And he's actually writing?'

'He is; I've never seen his hand move so fast across the

page.' I shall have trouble deciphering it for copying, I'm thinking.

'He has a need to hurry.' Tom snickers. He puts down his bowl and begins to scratch his chin. 'Bennet has lost patience with him. He and Nashe and Hobbes are off calling on the theatres to see if any of the companies are in need of actors.'

'They intend on leaving Master Waller?' I stop in my task, shocked. 'And you?'

'I go where Bennet goes, being his apprentice. Though we won't get any good parts in a big company, as we'll be last in.'

'Master Waller pays you; why would you leave?' I ask.

'Master Waller doesn't pay me; he pays Bennet and Bennet pays me.'

I nod, though I do not quite see the difference.

Tom throws up his hands and sighs at my ignorance. 'I've been with Bennet since I was ten. Bennet is my master; he taught me first to play the children's roles and then he trained me in the art of playing women. And when my voice breaks he'll show me how to act the man. After that my apprenticeship ends and I must find my own way. Until then I am with Bennet.' This last said proudly.

'But what of Master Waller? Do you owe him nothing? Does Bennet owe him nothing? Hobbes? Nashe? They'll just abandon him?' I feel the panic rise in my throat.

The other day in the yard of the George Inn, when the actors spoke so scornfully of Master Waller's work, I had thought it little harm for I did not believe they meant the half of what they said. Now here they are, trying to find a way to leave him! It will be a humiliating blow for him. I shudder to think of how he will take it. What will he do if they leave? Will he give up? Will he dispense with my services too? What will I do then? Where will I go?

'You are Waller's Men!' I say.

'We're actors – we have to act! In this house Master Waller's the only one who gets to play a role – he's acting the playwright!' Tom shrugs, and slumps against the wall. 'He has land in Sussex which provides him with a living. He can indulge himself in this pretence. What about us? We're left idle most of the time when we should be on the stage. And Bennet, as the lead actor, should be taking part of the profits from performances too, but there's no profits to be had, are there?' He idly stops a passing beetle with his left foot and watches it turn itself about and scuttle the other way. 'Nashe said we'd rue the day we made this deal with Waller. He always said no good would come of being paid to do nothing.'

He halts the beetle with his right foot, and the beetle turns again. He lets it reach his left foot one more time, then grinds it under his heel.

'Flea! The master's shouting for you,' Annie calls from the kitchen. 'I hope you have the quills done. He sounds uncommon excited.'

I leap up in such a hurry I spill the lot about my feet. I gather them up again – no thanks to that layabout Tom – and hare on up the stairs. I'm given a sheaf of foul sheets in exchange for the quills, and orders to find somewhere to begin making fair copies of them.

'Tell Annie I said you are to have a corner of the kitchen table to work on.' Master Waller doesn't wait for my reply nor see the worry in my eyes. He's humming a little ditty to himself. He knows not that his household is shifting underneath him.

I open my mouth to speak; he closes the door.

I scan the pages as I descend the stairs. Behold the Moon it says on the top sheet. That's not the name it had before. I check the list of characters – they are all different. He's not rewriting what he tore up the other day; he's begun something entirely new.

'A new play, the whole first act,' I say to Tom and Annie when I reach the kitchen.

Tom pulls a face that could be surprise or disbelief. He comes inside again and sits down while I read. Though Annie goes on stirring her pot, she never takes her eyes off my face as I read through the first scene.

It's good, I think. It starts strong and fast. There are twists and turns but I can follow it. And I want to follow; my eyes are chasing the words like a dog chases rabbits. Is it really good, though, or do I just want it very badly to be so? What know I of plays? I pass the pages to Tom.

'Is it worth reading?' he asks.

'It's not as good as the play we saw the other day,' I venture. 'But...' I hear the quaver in my voice.

Tom hears it too and snatches up the sheets. Now Annie

and me are watching Tom, who reads slowly, so slowly I'm fairly hopping in my seat.

'It's good, isn't it?' I whisper.

Tom nods.

'Read it to me,' says Annie, and Tom obliges. He changes his voice with every part. He's good, is Tom, and Annie forgets the stew. We none of us notice shadows at the back door; we're caught up in the action and the words. When Tom reaches the end of the act we clap loudly.

'What will Bennet say to this?' I ask, thinking happily that Master Waller is saved the mortification of losing his actors now.

'He'll say well done to Master Waller that he's finally turned his pen to good use,' says Bennet from the doorway. 'More's the pity it's too late!'

'What d'you mean "too late"?' asks Tom.

Bennet, Hobbes and Nashe come in the kitchen, all three with faces so gloomy you'd think they'd come a-mourning.

'We've made a tour of the theatres north and south of the Thames. The Curtain said they might have casual work for one of us, the Rose likewise. None will take all four of us together,' Hobbes growls. 'But worse than that, and all unbidden, they each said how we'd best take what work we can get as they wouldn't stage another Waller play, not if Master Waller bought up every seat in the house himself.' Hobbes rips a piece of bread from a loaf Annie has placed on the table. 'Money can't buy our playwright everything, it seems,' he adds, and rams the bread into his mouth all in one go.

Nashe purses his lips. 'Master Henslowe at the Rose said the few folk who came to our last play were the roughest of the rough, that it was more like to bear-baiting than to theatre. 'Twas not just the lack of tickets sold that he complained of but all the drink and food sales lost as well.'

'But if Master Henslowe was to read this,' I say, snatching up the new sheets. 'Surely then—'

'He'll not read it,' Bennet says, his temper near his teeth. 'He scoffed at us for working for a fool. His actors were snickering and throwing us pitying looks.'

'They said the same at the Swan?' Tom asks desperately. 'The Theatre, too?'

'Them all, I tell you,' roars Bennet, picking up a stool and flinging it through the open door where it lands amongst the chickens and sets them all a-squawking.

He stalks about the kitchen. We all breathe in and press ourselves against table or wall to give him room to walk his anger out. I think it best to keep the pages of the play close to my chest in case he turns on it and flings it to the chickens as well.

'What if...?' The words creep out despite me. I try to bite them back.

Bennet rounds on me, that smile starting on his face. 'What if what, Bacon?' he sneers softly. 'Pray tell us what stupendious thought your pickled country sausage of a brain has thrown forth.' Tom lays a warning hand on my arm. Annie silently removes the clay jug from the table.

'The George Inn,' I stammer. 'Didn't it used to put on plays?'

'The past tense is the correct one to use, Bacon. Are you suggesting we turn back tyme to, O, 1570?'

'Mightn't they be prepared to, just this once—?'

'No, they might not,' he snaps. 'They have no licence to put on plays, not since the theatres were built. Think again.'

I chew my lip. 'What if it was like the other day?' I ask. Bennet glares at me.

'What if we were – you were – to sit about the inn yard like any other customers, then begin the play as if by chance – as if it was just another conversation but louder than the rest?'

'Go on.' Bennet frowns and becomes still.

'The other day when you jumped up on the table, the crowd all stopped to watch. They enjoyed the entertainment; how much more would they enjoy a whole play, given them for free?'

'And what's the point of it, if it's for free?' Hobbes splutters. 'What's in that for us?'

'We find a way to bring—' I start.

'Master Henslowe to the scene,' Bennet shouts. 'And Master Langley and old Burbage. They hear the play, realise its merits and fight over which theatre has the pleasure of producing it. Ha! Our Flea is not such a bacon after all!'

He claps me on the back so hard my ribs bash off the table and Act One spills to the floor. Tom and me dive *underneath and gather it up, me blushing with pleasure and relief.*

The actors will not leave!

Master Waller's play may yet be performed!

I am not such a bacon after all!

Above our heads the three men are already making plans, dividing up the roles and devising ways to tempt the theatre owners into attending.

SEVEN

'Never step backwards without looking, Claudine. Try and fix that in your mind and it'll keep you safe up on deck *and* behind the stage,' Eoin said as he climbed the steps which rose on the starboard side of the theatre and slid into the third row of seats. 'Nette will be your main trainer for the summer, though everyone will be happy to help.'

Claudine nodded and Nette smiled at her encouragingly. Lally wandered up the steps to sit beside Eoin. On the way she peeked out of a porthole.

Where was the boy? He'd disappeared outside straight after breakfast.

'How much experience with puppets do you have, Claudine?' Nette asked.

'My grandpère left me his puppets, two beautiful *fin de siècle* marionettes.' She pulled her phone out of a pocket and briskly clicked and scrolled. 'He taught me a little when I was a child but I have never been involved in a professional performance.' She held out the screen and showed them some photos of a Pierrot and Pierrette.

'Ooh, nice!' Eoin said. 'Your grandfather was a puppeteer?'

'Yes. He travelled with a small theatre group when he was young, doing shows around villages in northern France, before the Second World War. After that, not so much, just occasional shows – at Christmas, for birthdays.'

'So, it's in your blood then.' Eoin looked impressed. 'What do you work at, Claudine?'

'I'm an art teacher but I have always, always wanted to do this, to train with puppets and, perhaps, work with them at weekends and during the summer, you know?'

'Let's get you started then!' Eoin said. 'First, come up here into the pews and look at the stage from the audience's perspective.'

Claudine sat beside Lally and Nette went backstage.

'It looks quite large from here,' Eoin explained, 'and when the puppets are onstage–' Stork appeared from one side and flapped slowly into the centre '–they look bigger too. But it's a bit of an optical illusion, as you'll see in a minute. The audience become focused on the stage and are unaware of the space above it, the two bridges on which the puppeteers are working.' He pointed to the large black expanse of wall above the stage opening which hid the puppeteers from view.

'Which is how it should be!' Nette's voice came from about where Eoin was pointing.

'Which is how it should be.' Eoin nodded. 'We're traditionalists here on the *Beetle* – we don't believe in the operators being seen onstage with the puppets. Some folk think that's old-fashioned of us, but we feel the focus should be on the puppets themselves. The audience should never be aware of the hands on the strings.'

Claudine did her mouth shrug thing which, Lally thought, could mean pretty much anything.

'OK,' Eoin said. 'Let's get you working a puppet.'

As the Frenchwoman went behind the little stage Eoin settled onto the bench, stretching his long legs out over the seats in front. 'Let's see if her grandpère taught her as well as your père taught you,' he whispered, poking Lally in the ribs with his elbow.

'Big-head,' she whispered and poked him back. She settled against him in the seat and waited.

There was some rustling and a few exclamations, then the sound of Claudine climbing the ladder. A murmur of voices as Nette explained the safety rails and the best way to move about up on the bridge. Then Bear joined Stork onstage. There were more murmurs and Bear began to jerk about, which Lally knew meant Nette was showing Claudine the correct way to hold the control.

'Ah, *oui*, yes,' Claudine said, and Bear straightened up and began to show signs of life.

Lally jigged about in her seat impatiently. Eoin hummed quietly to himself. 'Give her a few minutes to find her fingers,' he said.

Tac. Something small must have hit the roof just

above their heads. Lally looked up, but Eoin ignored it.

'S'nothing,' he said, keeping his eyes on stage. 'A twig falling.'

Tac.

'Here we go.' Eoin straightened up a little as Bear began to walk across the stage, unsteadily at first, then with slightly more assurance.

Tac. Tac. Tac.

What was that noise? Was it Gilles? What was he doing?

Lally leaned towards the nearest porthole and craned her neck to look up and down the towpath. To her right she just caught a glimpse of jean-clad legs on the gangplank. They stepped onto *Beetle* and out of her view. Blue jeans, washed out and ripped at the knees.

Gilles's jeans were black. And it wasn't Des either. Lally frowned. People often came nosing around looking at the barge, but they usually knew to stay off the *Beetle* if she wasn't open for business. She stood up and pressed her face to the glass to get a better view.

OK, the legs were back. Whoever it was was leaving.

But there was something odd about the way the legs were moving. They were creeping, as if they were trying not to make a noise.

She could see him properly now as he stepped back onto the towpath. A man, young, scruffy, with something heavy in his arms.

'Eoin!' She turned back to the theatre. 'Someone's nicking our woodpile.'

'What?' Eoin scrambled to his feet.

'A man. I think he's stealing the wood.'

Eoin shot to his feet and scrambled quickly over the seats in front. He jumped the last bench and tore off along the passageway towards the stern. Lally heard him thump up the stairs and throw open the door.

'Hey! What you think you're playing at?' he roared.

Looking back out the porthole Lally saw the legs stop mid-creep, swivel, turn again and break into a ragged run. She ignored Nette's startled 'What's going on?' and raced after Eoin, arriving on deck in time to see the man drop his load as he scarpered up the steps to the road above. By now Eoin was close behind and had to jump to avoid the tree trunk he'd pulled out of the canal the other day as it came tumbling down. It caught him on the legs and he fell forwards, still shouting at the thief and shaking his fist.

'Are you all right, Eoin?' Lally ran to his side.

'I'm fine, fine, grand.' He sat on the bottom step and rubbed his shins. 'Damned if he was getting this lump of wood after all the trouble it gave us,' he said. 'Go do your own dirty work,' he yelled up at the street, though the man must have been well out of earshot by this time. He ran his hand over the trunk.

'It's dry. Would you believe that? It's only been out

66

of the water a couple of days.' He looked at it more closely. 'It's not half so rotten as I thought it was either. Ow!'

He yanked his hand back. 'Blasted splinter,' he said, twisting his wrist up to his mouth and sucking it. 'If ith waff in a liffle beffer shaff ith wou wake a wovly wuppet,' he said.

'What?' Lally asked.

Eoin took his wrist away from his mouth. 'If it was in a little better shape it would make a lovely puppet,' he repeated, stroking the wood again. 'Pity.'

'Here's Des,' Lally said, spotting the older man coming towards them along the canal path. 'Des, someone tried to steal our wood. Eoin ran after him and he dropped it.'

'Must have been a right eejit if he thought he was going to get that lump of wood up those steps on his own. Either that or he was desperate. You should have let him have it,' Des said, squatting down to look at the wood more closely. 'I'm thinking it's hawthorn. Unlucky wood, if my old gran was to be believed.'

'What do you mean, unlucky?' Lally asked, frowning.

Des scratched his chin. 'I remember bringing a branch full of flowers indoors when I was a chisler and my gran nearly had a fit. She wouldn't have mayflower in the house. That's what she called it – mayflower. She said it was sacred to the faeries and to be left well alone.'

Lally suppressed a gasp. She remembered the strange

face she'd seen in the water. But that had just been her mind playing tricks, right? It still gave her the creeps when she thought about it.

'Will you help me get it down below, in case that lad comes back?' Eoin asked Des. 'We can stick it in a corner of the chow house.' Des nodded and grabbed one end of the trunk.

'What about what Des's gran said?' Lally asked, trying not to sound anxious. 'About it being unlucky to bring indoors?'

'Old wives' stuff.' Eoin snorted. 'One thing I know: it's a decent bit of firewood that we'll not be sorry to have this winter and I'm not losing it to some passing chancer.'

Lally nodded, but she couldn't help giving a little shiver.

You're too old to believe in faeries, Lally McBride, she told herself. Grow up.

'Any chance you'd lend me a sketchpad and some drawing pencils?' Eoin said, still looking at the wood.

'Sure,' said Lally. 'Why?'

'I have an idea for a puppet I'd like to sketch.'

'You'll not be making it with this, Eoin,' Des said, eyebrows raised. 'It's not in as bad a shape as I thought it was the other day but it's still not good enough for carving.'

'I know, I know.' Eoin nodded, absentmindedly stroking the trunk again. 'But it's given me an idea ... so maybe you could get me that sketchpad now, Lal?'

'Aye, aye, Captain. Right away, Captain.' Lally saluted and clacked her heels together but Eoin was too busy looking at the wood to respond. She left him and Des heaving the trunk between them and headed towards the *Beetle*.

Tac.

The noise – it was still there. Lally's eyes looked for the source. A jackdaw was on the roof, midship.

It was never the one from the other day – from the Islington Tunnel? Nah, couldn't be. Jackdaws were ten a penny. Just a coincidence.

It had something small in its beak and as Lally stared at it, it dropped the little thing and launched itself skywards. Lally stepped onto the *Beetle*'s gunnels and reached across the roof to see what it had been playing with.

A wee peeble. What had it wanted that for? Had it mistaken it for a snail?

Lally bit her lip. Whatever the silly bird was up to it had drawn her attention outside at just the right moment to stop that creepy old bit of wood from being nicked. And she knew she was being silly but after what Des had said about it being unlucky, she couldn't help wishing that it *had* been stolen.

EIGHT

S omeone was behind the stage; Lally recognised the sounds. She'd come into her cabin after dinner and started reading her book. She must have dozed off still fully clothed. A glance at her watch told her it was half nine. She sat up and listened.

It wasn't anyone who knew their way around; they were making way too much noise. Must be Claudine, getting in a little more practice. Lally settled back onto her pillows.

No.

Nette had suggested to Carla and Des that they take Claudine to the Prince Alfred for a drink; they'd hardly be back yet. Eoin had stayed behind – he was in his cabin, sketching.

Lally sat up again.

She leaned forward and quietly opened her door a crack. *Tap tap tappity tap.* The unmistakable sound of a puppet being walked across the boards. She slid off her bed. Her cabin was right behind the stage area and through the door she could see that some lights were on and Bear was taking a rather clumsy stroll through the forest. So it must be Claudine after all; she'd come back early.

Not bad, Lally thought. The walking movement was OK for a beginner, but the head was all over the place.

She came through the doorway and reached the ladder that led to the front bridge.

'Hey,' she said as she began to climb, 'would you like me to show you…'

But it wasn't Claudine; it was the boy, Gilles. Lally had been watching out for him all day, wanting to meet him properly, not sure what she'd say to him when she did. At dinner he'd been sitting at the other end of the table and she'd heard him occasionally speaking to Carla. Afterwards he'd wandered off outside, his head bent over his iPad.

He didn't turn his head now, remaining hunched over the leaning rail, arms out, staring down at Bear below him. Lally hesitated. He probably wanted to be left alone.

'*Oui*,' he said.

'Um – what?'

'*Oui*. I'd like you to show me how to work the puppet.'

'Oh. OK.'

All the puppets that were being used for the summer show were hanging in the wings. Lally unhooked Wolf and settled her fingers into their familiar positions on the control. Out of the corner of her eye she saw the boy staring at her hands as he adjusted his.

She slipped the index finger of her free hand into the small plastic ring at the top of Wolf's nose-string. She moved her finger slightly and below them Wolf nodded his wooden head. The boy copied the movement and Bear nodded shakily back.

'Good evening,' Bear said in a low growly voice.

'Good evening,' Wolf replied, and raised one hand in salute.

Bear slowly raised his.

Wolf bowed low. 'Pleased to meet you,' he said shyly.

Bear dropped his head slightly. 'Me too,' he growled.

OK, Lally thought. What now? What do I do? What do I say?

She offered Wolf's paw and Bear held out his. As the two paws met, the strings tangled ever so slightly. Lally pulled Wolf's paw clear and backed him up then walked him jauntily away.

'Walk with me, Bear,' she said. Bear grunted and followed with a heavy plodding gait.

'Did you hear that?' Wolf stopped suddenly. He stamped his hind feet. Bear did a double-take.

'Someone's coming!' Wolf said.

'Let's hide in the trees,' growled Bear and shuffled over to the little plywood forest. Wolf hurried after him.

Behind the trees Wolf breathed heavily, and looked about him. Bear became still. Lally stole a sideways glance at Gilles. His face was set in the serious frown he'd arrived with yesterday.

'You don't want to be here?' Wolf asked, tipping his

head over to one side. 'In London, I mean.'

Bear attempted a shrug. 'I'm not supposed to be here.'

'You'd prefer to be with your dad,' Wolf said.

'No. But I would prefer to be in Paris,' Bear grumped. 'I'm missing out on the last term in school.'

'That's a bad thing?' Wolf sounded astonished. Lally couldn't imagine liking being stuck in the same room all day, sitting behind a desk.

Bear laughed. 'No. But I'm missing football practice. And my friends. I've nothing to do here but be in the way.'

'You're not in the way,' Wolf protested, waving his forepaws in the air.

Bear snorted and slumped in a messy heap.

Change the subject, Lally thought. Ask him something else.

'What did you do today?' Wolf asked, sitting down beside Bear.

'Wandered about. Read a book on my iPad. Drank coffee.'

Drank coffee? Lally had never liked the taste of coffee.

'Doesn't sound so bad.' Wolf's ears flipped upright.

'No. But four months of it will drive me crazy.' Bear's head sank between his shoulders.

'I suppose.' Wolf lowered his ears sympathetically.

'Have you always lived on the barge?' Bear sat back up.

'Mm-hm.' Wolf nodded.

'Cool,' said Bear as he clumsily stood up again and began to walk away. 'Have you always worked the puppets?'

'As long as I can remember.' Wolf jumped up, brushed himself off, and followed. 'I was four when I first came up here on the bridge and eight when I did my first show.'

'Eight?' Bear spluttered, turning so quickly that Wolf ran into him and paws and strings jumbled hopelessly together.

'Don't move,' Lally said. 'Don't do anything. I'll get down and fix it. Here.' She held Wolf's control out to Gilles.

'It's all right, I've got it.' The voice below them made them both jump. Eoin's head appeared as he leaned in from in front of the stage and began to gently unwind the strings. He glanced up at Gilles.

'Seems you're a quick study and we're a trainee short this year. You'd be doing us a favour if you were to step in. There.' He stood back and the puppets swung apart. 'What do you say?' He looked up again.

'I – um – *mais oui*, yes!' The boy's face broke into a slow smile. 'Yes. That would be very good.'

'Welcome to the company.' Eoin held out his hand and Gilles reached down to shake it.

'Thank you,' Gilles said. 'Thank you very much.'

'No problem,' Eoin said. 'Can't have you going crazy

now, can we?' He laughed and walked away into the dark.

Lally and Gilles looked at one another. His brown eyes were sparkling. He's rather good-looking when he's not frowning, Lally thought.

'How long do you suppose Eoin was watching us?' Gilles asked.

Lally shrugged. She dropped her gaze to the two puppets below them.

'Rehearsals nine sharp tomorrow morning!' Eoin's voice boomed back from the chow house. 'Long day's work ahead, you two. Get some kip.'

'Kip? What is kip?' asked Gilles.

'Sleep!' said Lally.

'Kip,' said Gilles, nodding. 'I will get some kip.'

Lally giggled. Onstage, Wolf nodded goodnight to Bear before Lally lifted him into the air and hooked the puppet back onto one of the pipes. Gilles hung up Bear then swung himself easily onto the stage below. Lally dropped down to join him and they both stood for a moment smiling at each other, giants amongst the miniature trees.

'Goodnight, Lally,' Gilles said and held out his right hand. She held out hers and they shook rather awkwardly.

He smiled at her again and ducked his head down to exit through the stage opening.

'Goodnight, Gilles,' Lally said. She switched out the lights and stepped off the back of the stage.

'You were right, by the way.' Gilles voice came through the darkness. 'The hammock is really comfortable. See you tomorrow.'

'See you,' Lally said. She swung around the ladder, a smile still on her face as she closed her cabin door. Maybe this summer would be fun after all.

9th day of May, 1596

*T*he hush. That's what astonishes me most. The yard of the George Inn is full of people and more are hanging over the rails of the balconies on all three sides. Yet all is quiet, every eye and ear on the man and woman standing there, proclaiming their love for each other. The couple kiss, the crowd sighs. I blink back tears from my eyes. The actors bow, the crowd breaks into loud applause. Hobbes and Nashe join Bennet and Tom at the top of the yard. They all bow together. The audience are cheering, me along with them. I've never enjoyed a day so much as this, never felt such terror, such excitement!

The terror began with the walk from Master Waller's house to the George. The actors were already in their costumes, Bennet and Nashe dressed as noblemen, Tom dressed as a young lady and Hobbes dressed as her serving woman. They were breaking half a dozen sumptuary laws at once, what with dressing above their rank by wearing silk, velvet and embroidery, and in the colours scarlet, yellow and silver. Only Hobbes was clad in rough cloth in the dull hues allowed us ordinary folk – gown of goose-turd and cloak of rat.

But he and Tom being men dressed as women was what was most likely to bring the law down on our heads. Not that anyone seeing Tom dressed in a gown, dark tresses tumbling about his shoulders, face painted white, cheeks blushed with red, would know him for a boy, but Hobbes? Despite the costume and the periwig there is no mistaking he's a man.

'No one has yet been hanged for breaking a sumptuary law, Flea,' Bennet said. 'Besides, we actors have a dispensation to dress in costumes and play the fairer sex.'

A dispensation which only exists within theatre walls. I knew it and he knew it, but I held my tongue, ignored the stares of passersby and concentrated on carrying the heavy bag of props which I had charge of. When we reached the inn gates Bennet and Nashe went first. They walked briskly across the yard and disappeared into the inn itself. Tom and Hobbes found a shadowed spot just inside the gates, sat down and pulled their cloak hoods close about their heads. I went to take up my appointed place near where the action would be played out. I sat down and shoved my bundle under the table. A tankard of ale appeared in front of me without my asking; the innkeeper himself served it me with a wink.

I swear I thought I'd die of anticipation those few moments. My heart was thundering within my chest. I looked around the yard. Bennet had said it should be fairly busy, the theatres being closed of a Thursday afternoon, and he was right. There were at least fifty men and a few women at the tables but I recognised the two extra men *that Bennet had engaged for the performance to complete the cast. They ignored me and I looked away. I pretended to sip my ale as I peeked up at the centre balcony. It was empty. Any moment now, I thought, any moment…*

'The night is dark, your Excellency!' a voice proclaimed suddenly, and Nashe was there. His line was spoken like a quiet aside but carried clearly over all the beery babble. 'Yet the moon is faire and full.'

Down in the yard a few heads turned up towards the voice and there were some smothered giggles.

'The moon is faire, but the sea is wild. This ship tosses about like a leaf in a tempest.' Bennet and Nashe swayed from side to side as if the balcony was shifting under their feet.

Frowns, gawps, puzzled glances and mutterings. Some faces turned to stare up at the two men on the balcony; others seemed to study their ale.

'God speed us safely to shore. We must not fail in our task, good Edmunde. The assassins must not be allowed to succeed in their foul purpose.'

Backs stiffened, faces blanched. More folk openly looked upwards. Everyone was listening now but Bennet and Nashe disappeared as quickly as they'd come. The confused crowd had begun to mumble when a faire young maiden, obviously of noble birth, stood up at the other end of the yard and cried: 'Valentyne, will I never see you again?'

'Forsooth, 'twould be better for all if you'd never set eyes on that same Valentyne,' replied her huge serving maid, shaking her ugly head. ''Twill end in tears

and heartache; I feel it in my marrow.'

I think it was the sight of Hobbes that made the crowd tumble to what was going on. When they saw his height, his huge shoulders, the dark stubble on his chin breaking through the white make-up, and heard his baritone delivery, they began to guffaw. He played up the comedy, heaved his padded bosom and swaggered his farthingaled hips. That drew our first applause of the afternoon and one or two men ran out onto the street shouting, 'A play, a play, come see!'

Over the last two hours the inn has filled with so many bodies that there is scarce room for the players to perform. I've been running hither and thither with my bag, dispensing hats and moustaches to Nashe and the two other fellows, that they might fill several different roles without confusion. A hand mirror was needed by Tom in the second act, a dagger required by Bennet in the third. I've been hiding myself under the shade of the balcony and making sure I'm always where I'm needed. I am both the stagekeeper who provides the props, and the book-keeper who feeds lines when they're forgot, for I know the parts full well as the actors.

The audience, for that is what the inn crowd is become, laughed loud and hearty throughout the early scenes, then, as things took a tragic turn, were suitably distressed. The innkeeper and his staff have been run off their feet throughout, keeping their customers in ale and pies. And during Act Three, Scene Four, Tom whispered an aside to me that Henslowe, the owner of the Rose, is sitting on the second balcony.

That's where I look to now as the actors dance their closing jig, to music played by a fiddler the innkeeper has engaged. Henslowe's face is hidden from me. He is not clapping. He is standing up, pushing his chair away behind him. Another second and he'll be gone. I look back to the actors; their jig is done, one more bow and they disperse, all walking in different directions. I try to catch Bennet's eye but he is quickly surrounded by admirers. I push my way through the crowd to Tom.

'Henslowe,' I say. 'He's left his seat. I do not know where he is.'

Tom looks around anxiously, then points. Master Henslowe has entered the yard and is beckoning Bennet, who shrugs off the crowd and goes to him. Tom and I see Henslowe put his arm around the actor's shoulders and lead him to a corner. Hobbes and Nashe join Tom and me and we move to a table to watch and wait. Around us the inn crowd settle back to their seats or drift out into the street.

'Herring pie and as much Mad Dog as you can drink!' declares the innkeeper. 'A novel idea, well executed! I swear it was a good ten minutes before most of the crowd knew it was all an act they were witnessing. 'Twas like the old days, having actors working the yard.'

'You're not worried the Master of the Revels will come harassing you?' Nashe asks.

'I'm not! He may certainly point out I have no licence

to stage plays but since no one paid admittance I do not think he can do more than grumble. And Bennet got the play itself approved by him the other day. We've twisted the law, not broken it. Ha!'

In the corner Bennet and Henslowe rise to their feet. Henslowe holds out his hand and Bennet takes it. They both smile and Henslowe walks away.

'He's done it! He has a deal,' says Nashe, as Bennet comes towards us, beaming.

'Well?' asks Hobbes.

'Well?' asks Tom.

I am too nervous to speak.

'Behold the Moon is engaged to play the Rose,' Bennet says, taking a swig from my tankard. 'We are in luck, for Henslowe has a sudden gap appeared in his playlist which he urgently wishes to fill. We are to do three performances, beginning four days hence.'

The actors whoop and clap him on the back.

'Bennet, you're a clever one!' says the innkeeper.

'Ah, but 'twas not my idea that got us here.' Bennet grins and wipes ale from his beard. 'Our good Flea here must take the praise for that.'

'To Flea, then,' says the innkeeper, turning to me and raising his cup.

'To Flea!' Bennet laughs, and tweaks my ear.

They all raise their ales and I feel the colour flood my cheeks. I am thrilled by their praise but even more pleased to think that, though he may never know it, I have helped bring my master's play to the stage.

NINE

'Gets hot on the bridge, doesn't it?' Lally said as she and Gilles emerged from the barge into the late afternoon sunshine.

'Yes.' Gilles nodded, flapping his T-shirt with one hand and balancing his iced lemonade in the other. 'Especially with five of us up there at the same time.'

It was a week since Gilles and Claudine had arrived. Rehearsals were well underway and Eoin had appointed Lally as Gilles's puppet trainer so they were spending the mornings working together on his operating skills, then working side by side all afternoon at rehearsals. In return, Gilles was showing Lally how to use his iPad.

He and his mum had been shocked by Lally's almost total lack of computer knowledge, so Claudine had suggested Gilles teach Lally basic stuff about using the Internet. They were hijacking wi-fi from a nearby cafe and Lally's daily lessons began after rehearsals were done. They surfed the Internet looking up music and movies and books. It appeared they liked all the same things, especially books.

It's only the middle of May, Lally thought, and I already don't want this summer to end.

They sat down in their usual post-rehearsal spot, a

bench facing the water, a small distance from the barge, shaded by wall and trees.

'Eoin doesn't work the puppets, no?' Gilles asked as he took his first slug of lemonade.

'Sometimes,' Lally answered, sipping hers. 'Very rarely. He's a bit too tall for working up there. Anyway, his job is directing.'

'But Carla has been directing us all week.' Gilles raised his eyebrows at Lally over his glass.

'Um, yeah. Eoin's busy designing a new puppet or something.'

She frowned. It was a bit odd. Eoin always directed the plays but for the last few days he had been shut in his cabin, drawing. It wasn't as if they even needed a new puppet right now. She was pretty sure Nette and Carla were a bit put out about it; she'd seen them exchanging frowns when he disappeared into his cabin after meals.

'He has carved all the puppets you use? They are very beautiful,' said Gilles.

Lally smiled. 'Yes, they're all his. Des and Carla make the backgrounds and props, Nette makes the costumes.'

'And the plays you perform, who writes them?'

'Eoin. Well, he adapts stories for the stage, like this version of *Hansel and Gretel* we're doing.'

Gilles said nothing and drained his lemonade. Lally glanced at him.

'Don't you like the play?' she asked.

'It's OK,' he answered, fiddling with his glass.

'Only OK?'

'It's a bit ... old-fashioned.'

'Traditional,' Lally corrected. 'We are a traditional company, we put on traditional shows.'

Mouth shrug.

'What does that mean?' Lally could feel herself bristling.

'I just think...' Gilles looked at her and hesitated. 'Never mind.' He shook his head.

'I don't mind. You can say what you like.' Lally lowered her face to her lemonade. She could feel her cheeks flushing.

I do mind, she thought. I mind very much.

Hansel and Gretel was one of the company's standard shows. They'd put it on lots of times over the years. It was sweet and funny and ... and ... well, it was a perfectly good retelling of the tale.

Wasn't it?

Gilles put down his glass and pulled his iPad from its pouch. 'Today we'll set up a Facebook page for you,' he said.

'There's no point,' Lally said stiffly.

'I do not understand.'

'No point in teaching me any more computer stuff. I won't have anything to use it on.'

'But a tablet like this will be perfect for you.' Gilles waved it under her nose. 'On the barge you have no space to store books – this holds thousands of books. You're home-schooled – this is great for looking things up. You meet people from foreign countries every year – you can stay in contact with them on this.' He tapped the screen with his finger for emphasis.

'I'm sure it would be useful, but there's no point because there won't be any money to buy one for me,' she said. 'Eoin and Nette have mobile phones, otherwise we don't do computers and stuff on the *Beetle*. Maybe that makes us old-fashioned, but there it is.'

Gilles ran his finger across the screen. 'I have offended you, with what I said about the play,' he said. 'I didn't mean to. It's just...'

Lally bit her lip. She was being silly. She loved using the iPad and she *was* hoping to persuade Carla and Nette to get her one for birthday and Christmas combined. And Gilles had a right to his own opinion. Just because they liked lots of the same stuff didn't mean they had to agree on everything.

'Go on.' Lally set her face in what she hoped was a neutral expression.

'Well,' he began, looking at her a little anxiously. 'I suppose I just think that ... something can be traditional without being ... prosaic.'

'Prosaic? *Prosaic?*' Lally spluttered. She wasn't totally sure what it meant but she knew it wasn't good.

'Maybe I use the wrong word.' Gilles's eyes grew into two alarmed circles and he held his hands up in front of him. '*Ordinaire?* Ordinary?'

'Prosaic, ordinary. That's what you think of my dad's play?' Lally stared at him. The awful thing was, somewhere inside, way, way down, she knew that maybe he was right. Maybe *Hansel and Gretel* was very ordinary. Maybe a lot of Eoin's plays were. And maybe in the last year she'd been secretly thinking that the jokes were a bit clunky and some of the scenes were a bit slow. And maybe that's why audiences were a bit thin on the ground recently.

She blinked back sudden tears and scrambled to her feet so quickly her glass toppled from the bench arm and went crashing to the pavement. Gilles leaned down towards the pieces at the same time as she did and their heads crashed together.

'I'll do it,' she snapped. She snatched up the pieces of glass and walked away.

'Lally!' Gilles exclaimed. 'Please, Lally.'

'I'm fine,' she said without turning her head. She dumped the glass in a nearby bin. 'I'm going for a walk.'

Eoin came through the *Beetle*'s door just as she was marching past the barge. "Lally! Could you rap on *Bird* and ask Carla and Nette to come down to the theatre for a moment? And where's Gilles? Isn't he with you?' Eoin looked up and down the towpath. 'There he is. Gilles! There's a meeting with everyone down below. Can you come? Now? Great.'

Lally bent her head a little so Eoin wouldn't see she was upset and start asking questions, but she needn't have bothered. He disappeared back into the *Beetle* as quickly as he'd emerged. She stepped onto *Bird*, knocked on the door, and repeated Eoin's message.

'OK, sure,' came the replies. 'Be right there.'

Gilles reached *Beetle*'s gangplank just as she did.

'After you,' Gilles said, and stood back for her to pass him.

'Um, thank you,' she muttered without looking at him.

Downstairs Claudine and Des were already in the theatre; Carla and Nette arrived a moment later.

'Sit, sit!' Eoin was almost bouncing around in front of the stage, a sheaf of paper in one hand. 'Make yourselves comfortable. I've something I'd like you all to hear.'

Nette and Carla looked questioningly up at Lally who had settled herself several rows back. She shrugged and looked at Des who was sitting in the front. He shook his head. 'Search me,' he said. 'I've no idea what's going on.'

Every face turned to Eoin whose blue eyes were dancing with excitement. He waved the papers in his hand and cleared his throat.

'I know I've been neglecting my directing duties,' he began. 'And I know you've all been working hard rehearsing and everything. And I know this is a bit sudden and will need a bit of adjusting to ... but—' He took a deep breath. 'I've written a brand new play,' he said. 'I've written a brand new play and I'd like to read it to you.'

TEN

Lally had never seen her dad so nervous. He had read through the pages with all his usual energy; changing voices, his face expressing the emotions of the different characters, his free hand and his body sketching the movements of the puppets. Now he had finished and no one had said a word for at least thirty seconds.

'Well?' Eoin asked, staring anxiously from face to face.

Were those beads of sweat on his forehead? Did he look a bit pale? It was fantastic, what he'd written. Lally was bursting to say so out loud but she bit her lip. Maybe she just wanted to believe it was good because Eoin was her dad.

'Bravo! Bravo!' Claudine and Gilles began to clap at the same time, and then everyone else joined in, laughing.

'That's very fine, Eoin,' Des said quietly. 'The best thing you've ever done, in my opinion.'

'Lovely, Eoin, really lovely,' Nette exclaimed. '*The Children of Lir* – why have we never thought of doing that before? It will work so well on stage, it has such great visual elements – the lakes, the swans, the storms.'

'So sad,' said Claudine. '*Tragique!* I am heartbroken for the poor children turned into swans by their jealous stepmother. And your writing is so poetic, Eoin. So much better than the script for *Hansel and Gretel*. You should write everything the theatre performs.'

'I do.' Eoin gave her a half-smile, half-grimace.

'Oh.' Claudine hid her face in Gilles's shoulder. 'I have made the faux pas?'

Carla laughed. 'A small one. This new play is fantastic but obviously we'll have to do *Hansel and Gretel* this season so we'll just have to make do with performing the less poetic work of Eoin McBride for now. Really, Eoin, it is great; we should do it for the Christmas season.'

'Actually...' Eoin gave an apologetic grin. 'I was thinking we'd put it on *this* season. We've done *Hansel and Gretel* so many times over the years, we're getting stale. This would be fresh, vibrant, a challenge for all of us. And we could do it if we moved our first performance on two weeks.'

Lally gasped. That would mean organising and rehearsing a completely new play in three weeks. Was that even possible? In front of her Claudine and Gilles whooped and Gilles turned his head to grin at Lally. She half-smiled back.

'You can't be serious?' Carla said.

Nette and Des were frowning too.

'Eoin – really, you aren't serious?' Carla asked again, standing up and throwing her arms out.

He nodded. 'I'm completely serious,' he said. 'You know as well as I do that audience numbers have been dropping. We need to do something about that. We need to try something new, something we're excited about.'

He was smiling but Lally thought she heard a distinct edge of impatience in his tone, which wasn't like him. There was a muscle twitching in his left jaw.

'What about the puppets?' Carla spluttered. 'Where are we going to get all the new puppets from? What about the backgrounds? Props?'

'I've thought about that,' Eoin said. 'With new costumes and some hair changes we can fill a lot of the roles with puppets we already have. Gretel can become Finnuala, the eldest of the swan children. Prince Charming, Hansel and Little Boy Blue can be refashioned to become her three brothers. The woodcutter can be re-costumed into King Lir. If we spend this week making new costumes and backdrops, then the next two rehearsing, we can do this.'

'But what about when the four children are turned into swans?' Nette asked. 'Where are we going to find four swan puppets? And what about the stepmother who gets turned into a – what was it?'

'A "witch-of-the-air".'

'Where do we get her from?'

'I plan on making her out of the hawthorn trunk,' Eoin said.

'What?' Des exclaimed. 'The log we fished out of the

canal? Don't be daft, Eoin! You know that wood isn't good enough to carve. I've seen you looking at it and patting and petting it this last week, but wishing it good wood won't make it good wood, and well you know it.'

A tingle crept along Lally's spine. The hawthorn trunk had been propped in the corner of the chow house all week, ever since the attempt to steal it. She'd noticed Eoin's eyes straying to it during meals once or twice but she'd been too busy chatting to Gilles to think anything of it. Eoin couldn't really mean to try making something from it. Even she knew the wood wasn't in a fit state to carve.

'No, no, you're wrong!' Eoin was almost shouting now. 'Come and see,' he said, and walked out of the theatre area, beckoning them all to follow him up the passageway.

In the chow house he grabbed the tree trunk and dragged it towards the centre of the space, shoving the dining table out of the way with his other hand. 'Look,' he said, twirling the thing on its base.

The trunk was small, standing about as high as Lally's hip, and it was about as thick as her small waist. When Eoin touched it, some flakes of the outer layer fell away and the wood beneath showed a fine reddish-brown hue.

Like snakeskin, Lally thought, with a shiver. Like it's casting off its old self.

Des knelt to take a closer look at the trunk. He prodded it with his fingers and knocked on it all over, listening and examining as he went. He looked up at them, his eyebrows raised.

'I'm flummoxed,' he said. 'I could have sworn this was old wood, totally useless from being in the water a long time. Good for nothing but burning. I must need glasses.' He tried the weight of the tree trunk against his shoulder, lifting it slightly off the floor. 'Ouff! It's much heavier than I thought too.' He shook his head. 'You're right, Eoin. It's a lovely piece of wood. It should make a fine puppet.'

'I told you!' Eoin grinned and tugged the trunk out of Des' hands. He leaned it gently back in its corner.

'I could make the swans,' Claudine said suddenly. Everyone turned to where she and Gilles were standing, a little apart from everyone else. 'They should be made of wire, very light,' she said, making shapes in the air with her hands. 'Almost transparent, covered only with gauze, and feathers. I would really love to make them if you'll let me.'

Lally took a step backwards, away from the bits of tree skin on the floor, to where Gilles was. They watched the adults argue back and forth, discuss the details, shake their heads over the impossibility of it and suggest solutions to problems as they arose. Nette and Carla held out for a while, then just Carla. Eventually she reluctantly gave in.

'One week,' she said. 'One week to sort out costumes, new puppets and the stage. If we don't have it all ready to go into rehearsal by then we go back to *Hansel and Gretel*.'

'Even Eoin can't complete a puppet in one week, Carla, you know that,' Des said.

They all looked at Eoin.

'Des is right, it isn't enough time.' He bit his lip.

'We can't afford to lose half the summer season over this, Eoin. We can't go a whole month more without a performance.' Carla shook her head. 'This just isn't practical.'

Lally felt her heart sink and she realised she'd been looking forward to the new play. But she knew Carla was right. A quick glance at Gilles showed her he was disappointed too.

'Unless—' Nette smiled suddenly.

'Unless what?' everyone asked.

'We start rehearsals with a stand-in puppet – Cinderella, maybe? I know it isn't perfect but it would only be until Eoin has the new puppet done.'

'How long would that be, Eoin?' Carla asked, a hint of a smile on her face at last.

'Two weeks – two and a half max.'

Carla considered this. 'Seems we have a new play to organise, people,' she said at last. 'Don't know why you're all standing around doing nothing!'

Claudine clapped her hands together in delight. Nette slapped Eoin on the back and went to help Des gather up the puppets that would be needed. Eoin pulled Carla into a bear hug and winked at Lally and

Gilles over her shoulder. Gilles turned to Lally and held up one hand in high-five position. Lally brought her hand towards his and he caught it, laughing.

'We are going to do something special now,' he said. 'Do something worthy of your father's beautiful marionettes.' He squeezed her fingers and looked at her, his face suddenly solemn.

Lally knew he was thinking of their row earlier, knew he wanted everything to be OK between them.

And it was.

She nodded. 'Yes. We're going to do something special now.'

ELEVEN

'Get lost, you two,' Des suggested with a wink. 'Everyone's busy and there's nothing ye can do to help yet. Go have an afternoon off; probably the last chance you'll get in a while.'

It was the day after Eoin's big announcement and Des was standing in front of the stage, knee-deep in plywood. Lally and Gilles stepped over a piece he was shaping into waves and picked up their jackets. Claudine was onstage, sitting cross-legged, a selection of the puppets dangling around her face. She was studying them carefully and drawing quickly on the sketchpad in her hand. Rolls of wire and various white materials which she had purchased earlier with Carla were scattered about. She reached into her pocket as they passed and handed some notes to her son.

'Treat yourself and Lally,' she said absentmindedly and shooed them away.

As they went up the stairs they could hear the sound of sawing coming from Eoin's cabin.

'He'll be dividing up the hawthorn trunk into smaller pieces for carving,' Lally explained.

She wondered why Eoin was choosing to work in the cramped space of his sleeping quarters. He'd moved the hawthorn trunk into his cabin last night; Des had been going over to it all evening, touching it and looking at it, like he couldn't trust his eyesight. This seemed to irritate Eoin and Lally had noticed that tic in his left jaw again.

He usually carved his puppets out in the chow house; at least, that's how she remembered it. Maybe he just wasn't feeling confident enough to work in front of everyone. Though that didn't seem much like Eoin.

But then Eoin wasn't behaving much like Eoin this last week. He'd spent most of his time in his cabin, barely talking to anyone, lost in his own world. Lally was used to him being at the centre of everything – the biggest talker, quick to laughter, encouraging everyone to have a good time.

Well, it had been ages since he'd written a new play or carved a puppet. Maybe he'd always been like this when he was creating stuff. Maybe she just didn't remember.

Outside the weather had turned cool again and a wind blew down the canal into their faces as Lally and Gilles stepped off the *Beetle*. From *Bird* came radio noise mixed with the whirr of a sewing machine.

The whirring stopped dead.

'Ach, blast!' a voice exclaimed.

'Sounds like Nette just broke a needle or the thread has snagged,' Lally whispered to Gilles. 'She and that sewing machine are old enemies.'

'We need to escape from these crazy adults!' Gilles laughed.

Lally nodded. 'They *are* all a bit nuts today.'

Gilles grabbed Lally's hand and broke into a run. Under the blue bridge, up the steps, along the railings; they didn't slow to a walk until they were halfway along Blomfield Road.

Gilles looked at the narrowboats packed end to end along the canal.

'They're pretty,' he said. 'I like the painted bits. They're cool.' He pointed to a door on one barge and some panels along the side of another.

'It's a tradition, a way of painting done only on barges,' Lally explained. 'It's called "Roses and Castles".'

She pointed out some more examples on the next two boats. Flower pots, buckets and watering cans, all decorated with daisies and roses and chrysanthemums on dark green, red, blue and black backgrounds. Nearly every barge they passed had something painted on it.

'Do the people on these boats live here all the time?'

'Yup. Most of them.'

'Do they ever move?' He was looking at the towpath alongside the barges, filled with pot plants, patio furniture and barbeques.

'A lot of them will go travelling at some point during the year but this is their permanent mooring, where they spend most of their time.'

They pushed away from the railings and walked towards Café Laville. It was perched on the Maida Hill

Tunnel, straddling the water just above the opening. They went in the door and stood at the counter.

'Tea or hot chocolate?' Gilles asked.

'Hot chocolate, please!' Lally said.

'Two hot chocolates and—' They gazed into the glass case of cakes while the owner smiled and waited for them to decide what they wanted. 'One of those.' Gilles pointed at an éclair oozing cream and covered in coffee icing. 'And you?' he asked Lally.

She chose a raspberry cupcake covered with white chocolate cream and topped with pink and blue berries.

Gilles carried the tray and they sat down at a table by the large window overlooking the water. The canal stretched away from them back towards the pool.

'May I ask you something - how do you say - personal?' Gilles said suddenly.

'Sure.' Lally said. 'Of course.'

'Where is your mother?'

'Oh. I don't know,' Lally said, staring at her hot chocolate. 'She left when I was a baby, I don't remember her.'

'You are not interested in her?'

'A bit.' Lally looked at Gilles and shrugged. 'I mean, I am. Of course I am. There are lots of things I'd love to know about her. I guess I don't like to upset everyone by asking.' She paused. She'd never said this out loud before, never even let herself think about it too much. 'Um, I mean, they say I can ask anything I like but I can see it makes them all uptight when I do, so I don't. You know?'

Gilles nodded. 'My parents divorced two years ago and Maman always says, talk, talk, talk about it. Ask whatever you want. But if I do, she gets all worried, like she is doing something wrong.'

He rolled his eyes dramatically and Lally smiled. 'What about your dad?' she asked.

'Papa is a jerk,' Gilles said, taking up a knife and slicing through the éclair. Lally divided her cupcake as well and they swapped halves. 'Well, he was being a bit of a jerk before we left. He's OK most of the time, but he promises to do things then doesn't do them. He is always super busy and acts as if Maman is not, as if his work is more important than hers.' He shook his head and bit into his piece of éclair.

'But you were looking forward to spending the summer with him?' Lally asked, taking her first sip of hot chocolate.

'Not really.'

They both laughed.

'It's important to Maman to do this training course with your company. She had to apply for time off work, organise a replacement, lots of stuff and, because I had to come along at the last moment, it nearly didn't happen.'

'That wasn't your fault, it was your dad's,' Lally reasoned. 'And it's all worked out fine anyway.'

Gilles pulled one of his now-familiar mouth shrugs.

100

Lally was getting better at reading them. There was a whole range. Some were smile substitutes, some sympathy, some indicated confusion, and others, she thought, indicated disagreement without actually saying so.

What did it mean this time? That he was happy being here? Would he still rather be at home in Paris?

'My friends are jealous of me already because I get to miss a month of school,' he said slowly, as if he was thinking it over very seriously. 'And when I get home I will impress them with stories of how I spent the summer living on a barge, working with puppets. They will have done the usual things. *Moi?* I will have done the coolest thing of all.' He grinned at her. 'So, yes, I would say everything is working out fine.'

Lally blinked. There were people who thought living on a barge was cool? And Gilles was one of them?

Gilles pulled his iPad out of his bag. 'Right.' He tapped it a few times and swiped the surface with his hand. 'Let's make you that Facebook page. So you can stay in touch with the other trainees you've met. So you can stay in touch with me.'

Lally smiled at him.

'You've got a hot chocolate moustache!' Gilles drew a finger in front of his mouth to illustrate. Lally reached into her pocket to get a tissue but before she could find one, Gilles had picked up a serviette, reached over and wiped it across her lip. She felt a blush begin across her cheeks and shook her hair forward so he wouldn't see, but he had already turned back to the screen.

'What are you going to call yourself? Lally McBride or Lavender Hale-Bopp?' he asked with a grin.

'Can we do something else first?' she asked. 'There's this thing I want to look up.'

'OK.' Gilles hit a search engine. 'What'll I type in?'

'Hawthorn,' Lally said, and took a bite of the raspberry cupcake. 'Hawthorn folklore.'

14th day of May 1596

*T*his afternoon is the second performance of *Behold the Moon* at the Rose Theatre. It played to a full house yesterday and will again today. Two thousand five hundred people each time!

The actors are out all hours. I hardly see them. No more performances for me. Master Waller is halfway through another play and I am set to making fair copies of it. I miss the hurly burly of the acting but Bennet has charged me with ensuring Master Waller writes but does no tearing. He says he depends on me for this. I will try to do his bidding but, as the master will not let me sit at my old desk in his work chamber any more, I'm not sure how I'll know if a tearing fit comes upon him. Meanwhile Annie must put up with me in her kitchen and I must try to keep flour and fat and blood off the sheets.

Mindful of my promise to Bennet I keep a sharp look out for signs of change in Master Waller, for any ill temper or despair in his demeanour. As well as refusing me entrance to the work chamber, I notice that he speaks to me less often. I try not to dwell on my worries about the hawthorne trunk, which is still in his chamber, for as Bennet keeps pointing out, the Master has had nothing but good luck since it arrived. Nonetheless, I can't help but observe that Master Waller used to tell me something of the history and science which he means to thread through his work – and now he barely speaks to me at all.

'I think Master Waller is taken to drinking,' I say to Tom and Bennet, first opportunity I get. 'His skin has an odd pallor, his breath smells strange. He won't let me within the work chamber for more than a moment and Annie says he won't let her in to clean it.'

Tom just shrugs. His skin has an unhealthy pallor too, now that I look at him. I suppose he hasn't cleaned all the make-up off from yesterday's performance. He yawns and slouches against a wall. Bennet yawns too but his eyes are twinkling and he stretches his limbs like a cat waking in the sun.

'You think Waller is imbibing? Good! He was far too temperate for my liking!' He laughs. 'If he has found drink he has also found his voice. No playwright ever wrote with a dry pen, my fine Flea.' He snorts at his own joke.

'You charged me to watch Master Waller and tell you if I saw anything that made me fear him turning on his work,' I say, a little stung by his tone.

'Fiddle-faddle! It sounds as if all change in him is for the better! Do not fret yourself, Flea! All's well!'

I bite my tongue and say no more.

I'll keep my worries to myself. Better still, I will stop looking for things to worry about now Bennet seems to have lost interest. My mother always says I fret over nothing, that I see problems where none exist.

When next I call at Master Waller's door to deliver him a new bunch of sharpened quills, I see he has taken the tree trunk – which never was used for the play – as his seat.

Old wives' tales; a tree is but a tree, I tell myself. Do not be such a bacon!

But then I observe something which worries me much despite my best resolve. It is a warm day, and Master Waller has his shirt sleeves rolled up. All about the inside of his lower arms are strange marks – black, congealed spots. I stare at them; he catches my gaze and hurriedly tugs his cuffs down to his wrists.

'Off with you,' he says, roughly shoving the new pages at me. 'Get on with your work and stop idling.' He slams the door shut in my face.

TWELVE

L ally was dreaming of thunder. Roll after roll after roll, breaking in waves around her.

She turned over and buried her head in her pillow.

Rrrrraaarr!

She blinked awake.

Rrrraaarrrraar! Aaaar!

With a giggle she realised it was just her stomach grumbling. She lifted her left arm towards the porthole and raised her new hessian blind. Squinting in the street light's glow, she checked her watch. Two in the morning.

Rrrar!

All right, all right, she thought. I'm hungry, I get it.

Lally hauled herself upright and felt along the wall for her hoodie. It was hanging in its usual spot but a quick check of the pockets only turned out a balled-up tissue, a fifty pence coin, and a crumpled chocolate wrapper. No actual chocolate, not even one square.

She sat in the dark trying to visualise the current contents of the *Beetle*'s fridge. Hmm. Some cheese. And there should be some of that ham left, if Des hadn't scoffed it all. And there might also be some of those yummy sticks of bread Claudine had appeared with yesterday in the breadbin.

She rubbed her hands together. One midnight sandwich coming up! She tugged the hoodie on over her pyjamas and scrambled off her bunk. Easing the door open, she slipped through into the theatre.

Maybe Gilles would be awake too.

But no. He was gently snoring in his hammock above the seats, his sleeping bag drawn up over his head. She cleared her throat and shuffled about a little.

Nope. Fast asleep. Solo sandwich then.

She tiptoed along the passageway towards the chow house where a small lamp was glowing, left on at night to guide the visitors to the head.

I think there's half a hard-boiled egg from the day before yesterday too, she thought, licking her lips. But I don't suppose there's any chance of lemonade. Water will have to do—

What was that?

She stopped in the chow house and listened. A gentle, steady tap-tapping. Coming from Eoin's cabin. She recognised the sound immediately; he was carving. Inside his room, she knew, a puppet was being fashioned, slowly, limb by limb. Curls of wood were falling away to reveal an upper arm, the torso, a hand, a foot. Eoin would be ankle-deep in the fragrant chips, mallet striking chisel so quickly it would appear as if the emerging creature was being freed from the wood. He would only slow the chisel down when it came to fashioning the features on the face, especially the eyes.

Maybe her midnight feast didn't need to be solo after all. She checked her watch again. Ten past two in the morning. A crazy time for Eoin to be working. He had to be hungry. She moved over to his door and raised a hand to knock. A strong scent enveloped her so suddenly it made her hesitate.

Wood, yes, but also ... wild garlic. Wet ferns and ... bluebells. It was so strong she swayed slightly, almost losing her balance. She shook her head to clear it and the smells were gone.

Or the illusion of them.

Bluebells! There couldn't be bluebells! Unless Eoin had taken to keeping pot pourri in his room. She raised her hand again to knock. Again her knuckles stopped, a whisper from the surface of the door.

Was that music?

Some sort of New Age meditation music, winding all over the place, imitating the wind. A woman's voice, high and reedy, warbling in some foreign language – Gaelic? Eoin's taste in music was definitely getting a bit strange.

Lally began to giggle but it caught in her throat.

Was it her imagination or was that light bleeding around the edges of the door actually pale green?

This is pure weird, she thought. Why can't I just knock on the door? She tried to lift her knuckles once more but her arm felt unaccountably heavy and she found her fingers sliding silently down the varnished surface back to her side.

'Eoin?' she said, but the name came out as a panicky whisper. She stared at her hand, trying to make it do what she wanted.

Knock on the door.

Why couldn't she do this?

There was that smell again.

A yawn split her face so wide it hurt and her eyelids began to droop. Why was she here? What had she got out of bed for?

'Bed,' she heard her voice murmur. Well, it had to be her voice. There was no one else here. 'Sleep. Sleep,' it was whispering.

She backed away from the door and stumbled into the chow house, clumsily rounded the table and lurched down the passageway towards the theatre. She held the wall for support; her legs seemed to have turned to jelly.

She must have sleep-walked the rest of the way because that was the last thing she could remember when she woke a few hours later.

Had she actually got up at all?

She sat up and tried to focus. Well, one thing was for sure, if the growls of her tummy were anything to go by – she never did have that sandwich.

Had it just been a strange dream? A *very* strange dream?

As her eyes adjusted to the early morning glow she

saw her cabin door was half open. She always shut her door. Always.

She sat there for a full five minutes, picking back over what she could remember and what she couldn't. The last bits were blurry, as if she had been in some sort of trance. Like the time she'd had a really bad cold when she was nine and Nette had given her medicine that tasted of cherries and made her drowsy.

It was no use. No matter how much she tried to grab at the edges of it she couldn't piece the bits of her night-time walk back together. They were all jumbled up and fuzzy and mixed up with dreams. She felt queasy and anxious and her head ached. She should go back to sleep.

But she didn't. Instead she reached over to the shelf where she'd put the print-out of the hawthorn stuff she and Gilles had looked up in the cafe a few days before. They'd found a lot of articles and Lally had cut and pasted bits from different websites and made a document out of it which they'd printed off at the local library when they'd finished at the cafe. There were about a dozen pages. She opened the porthole to let in some cool air, clicked on her lamp, took a deep breath and began to read.

Bad luck and faeries. Every site mentioned those words, even the proper historical sites with articles written by people with letters after their names.

The hawthorn was "strongly associated with the

faeries" and was a "marker to the faery realm". It was "bad luck to cut it for fear of offending the faeries that inhabited it". In medieval England it was considered safe to cut it in May but never any other month. Cutting it down at the wrong time was so unlucky that "the offender would lose his house, his children, or a limb".

And you should never bring the flowers indoors, like Des's gran had said. It brought death.

Lally pulled the duvet closer.

It's only folklore, she told herself. Silly superstitions.

She still wasn't sure what had happened to her earlier in the night but now her heart was thumping again and she was shivering. She probably shouldn't be reading this. It certainly wasn't helping her shake off the bad feelings she had about that lump of wood.

Hawthorn was strongly connected with Bealtaine, an ancient Celtic festival, one site said. And it was associated with fire, and with witches too, spirits called the hedgewitch, the hagwitch, the Thorn Lady or the White Goddess. They all had a double nature, a light, white side like the flowers of the tree, and a dark side like the sharp thorns. They might just as easily bestow wonderful gifts as bring terrible harm. Their animal familiars were crows and ravens.

Bad luck and faeries and witches.

We didn't cut the tree down, Lally reasoned, anxiously chewing at her fingernails. We rescued it from the canal, so none of the bad luck stuff will apply to us, will it?

But what about the faery and witch stuff?

Not that any of it was true. Of course it wasn't.

She chucked the pages back onto the shelf, clicked off her light and pulled the duvet up over her head.

Forget about it, she told herself. Go back to sleep. There's still an hour and a half before breakfast.

She wished she had never looked it up. She wished they'd never brought the wretched tree on board - it was giving her stupid nightmares.

And once Eoin made it into a puppet, it would be on board the *Beetle* for good.

21st day, May 1596

T *he arrangements in the house are thus: Annie sleeps*
in the kitchen, the actors bed down on the floor of
the hall. The master's bed chamber is up the stairs, across
from his workchamber. He sleeps in a four-poster bed and
I, as his apprentice, sleep on the trucklebed which rolls
out from underneath it. Because I share his bed chamber
I quickly notice that Master Waller is working later and
later into the night. Bennet says this is of no matter, that
writers must write whenever the spirit moves them. But the
nightmares that disturb Master Waller when he is abed,
the calling out, the shivering and sweating – is this all part
of it too?

The second play is writ and in rehearsal. It is even better
than the last. I press Bennet to convince Master Waller to
rest for a whyle before beginning another, to encourage
him to oversee the rehearsals. This goes well for three days
till Bennet can take the interference no longer, then Master
Waller disappears into his work chamber and takes up his
pen once more. Now he works only by night and sleeps
by day. He passes me the work to be copied as I rise for

breakfast and he makes his way to bed. He will not let me use the work chamber even when he is not in it. No one but myself and Annie think the master's actions strange.

'He's eating more than usual and yet he grows thinner,' she whispers to me, though there's no one else about to hear. 'There's vomit in his piss pot when I take it for emptying. I'm sure it's not my cooking has him ill.'

I assure her that I consider her cooking second only to my mother's and that it never upsets my stomach. (I do not mention that I've observed Tom puking after supper on occasion; I think Tom has a delicate constitution.)

'You wash Master Waller's shirts, Annie,' I say, thinking of the marks on his arms. 'Have you noticed anything strange about them?'

'Aye.' She nods vehemently. 'I think he must be attending the surgeon for something, for there are spots of blood and green pus all about the sleeves. The very devil they are to get out too.'

'You think he's being bled?' I ask, shivering at the thought.

'I do. The man has problems with his humours and many a physic will prescribe the letting of blood for that. Perhaps that has his stomach out of sorts?'

'Perhaps,' I say. But I do not think so.

Blood-letting was prescribed for my father in his final illness. I well remember the bowls full of red being taken away as my father grew whiter and lost what little grip he had on consciousness. I was eight years old. I sat at the foot of his bed like a little dog, thinking I could save him if

114

I just prayed often enough and hard enough, if I just made enough promises to God. A thousand wasted prayers and no promises to keep.

But that's no matter. 'Tis my opinion that Master Waller wouldn't be able to stand or walk about if he was being regularly bled. The marks on his arms are so many and so small – they do not put me in mind of my father's wounds. But something's not right. Master Waller is a changed man since ... since that thing was brought under this roof.

I am alone in the bed chamber now. I take my candle and carefully draw aside one curtain of the four-poster bed. It's so high I almost have to climb onto it to examine the sheets. Sure enough, there are spots of blood and greenish smears about the pillows and the linen.

What does it all mean? Is he drinking too much? If the evidence of my own eyes is anything to go by, he drinks less ale than anyone else in the household. Annie assures me that the whisky jar is no lower than it should be. I have stood as close to Master Waller as I can and smelled no drink upon him, only that strange sourness.

Annie says he's vomiting regularly. Is Master Waller ailing?

My granddam always warned us that to bring the hawthorne within was to invite death into the house.

I creep out into the corridor with my candle and stand outside the work-chamber door. I press my ear against it. There's Master Waller's voice. He's murmuring to himself.

My mother says that talking to yourself is the first sign

of madness. Bennet says that all writers talk to themselves. I do not know what to think. I'm turning to go back to my bed when I hear a sharp, half-stifled cry. My heart jumps to my mouth. I turn back and beat my fist upon the door.

'Master Waller,' I yell. 'Master Waller!'

By the time he comes to the door the whole house is awake and up the stairs. I stand surrounded by four bleary actors. Annie remains a few steps down, peering around Hobbes. The master only opens the door a tiny crack.

'What is it? Why do you disturb my work?' he asks.

'I – I heard you cry out, sir,' I stammer.

'Cry out? I was merely speaking aloud the part that I was writing to examine the sound of it,' he snaps and shoves the door to. I am left standing there surrounded by the sleepy actors, all glaring at me in confusion.

'There's something wrong with him,' I begin.

'There'll be something wrong with you,' growls Bennet, 'if you wake me up again at midnight. Who cares what he does in there, as long as the work is flowing? Leave what doesn't concern you, Flea. Leave it alone. Go back to bed, stop meddling.'

I trail off to my truckle bed but I know what I heard. And what is more, when Master Waller answered the door, I saw a drop of blood run down his wrist and drip off one of his fingers to the floor.

Bennet and the others do not care about the master, only that he produces good plays for them to act. But something is wrong, very wrong. My stomach is all twisted with foreboding.

I'll not leave it alone. If I could just get inside that chamber, I could see for myself what Master Waller does at night. If all he does is write, then what harm can there be in my watching over him in secret, just the once?

If what I do is meddling, I do it out of concern; I do it with the best of intentions.

With that thought I lay my head down and fall into a troubled sleep.

THIRTEEN

'A bit slow on the transition from children to swans, people,' Carla's voice called from the dark beyond the stage. 'But it's looking good; it'll look fantastic when we get the timing right. Let's go again, taking it from when Cinderella - I mean, the evil stepmother - casts the spell.'

Up on the bridge everyone giggled. Nette raised an eyebrow and beneath her on the stage Cinders shook her blonde tresses.

'You people aren't taking me seriously!' she huffed. 'I can play this role. Listen to me do the evil laugh thingy - mwhahaha!' She stamped her little pink foot.

'Positions, people,' Carla said, when everyone had stopped laughing.

On the front bridge Lally and Gilles switched places, passing close to each other as Gilles lifted his two children of Lir carefully over the two swan puppets Lally was working. Nette stayed put with Cinders over on stage left and on the back bridge Des and Claudine swapped with the remaining two children and swans.

The swan puppets were beautiful. The birds looked fragile but they moved wonderfully. Lally and Gilles had helped Claudine fashion the wings which were designed with hinges in the middle to allow them to fold like arms. Lally thought that gave them a human quality, making them look at once like birds and ballet dancers. The wings and heads were covered in tiny, snow-white feathers. The heads sat on necks which were divided into sections to allow for a variety of movements. Each bird had a red beak which could be opened and closed to give the appearance of singing.

The transition from children to swans involved a sort of dance amongst the plywood waves which Des had made for the first lake scene. When the witch cast her spell the audience would see the swans appear from the waves, embrace their corresponding child, then fly upwards towards the sky as the children sank below the water, their arms pitifully upraised towards the swans they were becoming.

The swans were much lighter than any puppet Lally had ever operated before and took a little getting used to. All of their expression would come from the movement of their necks and wings and everyone initially had trouble creating the elegant, wistful swan-moves Carla was demanding.

The last couple of days had been spent experimenting and getting used to the width of the puppets' wingspans. The accidental crashes and tangles during the flying sequences were becoming less frequent.

'But we haven't managed a single straight run-through of the whole show,' Gilles remarked to Lally. 'Is this normal?'

She shook her head. 'This is definitely much more complicated than the usual stuff we do.'

'But more challenging?'

'Sure.' She nodded. 'I'm learning new moves; we all are.'

'More challenging for the audience too,' Nette muttered.

Lally turned to look at her. 'You think?'

Nette nodded. 'I don't suppose that's a bad thing but it has Carla a bit worried. The story is really sad; what if the good folk of London don't like their puppet shows sad?'

'It is very beautiful,' Gilles said. 'Beautiful puppets, beautiful story, beautiful music.'

'I think you're right,' Nette said, grinning. 'Let's hope Eoin finishes the nasty stepmother soon because Cinders here just isn't up to the job.'

'Speak of the devil,' said Des.

A downward glance showed Lally Eoin's familiar blue sweatshirt and jeans just beyond the stage. In one hand he was gently holding something wrapped in a silk scarf. His other hand held a set of strings.

'Is it done, Eoin?' she called. She forced a little excitement into her voice. After the things she'd read she'd been hoping the wood wouldn't be usable after all.

His head appeared under the stage. 'It is, Lal.' He smiled up at her.

'Let's see!' Lally hooked her puppets on pipe, dropped

off the bridge onto the stage and reached a hand out to pull the scarf aside. Eoin twisted away from her.

'Let's get everyone down first,' he said. 'Come on, folks. I'll introduce you all to our new star.'

Gilles jumped down beside Lally; Des, Claudine and Nette descended the ladders and came around to the theatre area.

'You all grab seats out here and I'll unveil her on stage,' Eoin said.

He disappeared backstage as Lally and Gilles scrambled out into the theatre area and settled themselves into the front row.

There was the sound of feet on the ladder, followed by a muffled 'ouch'.

'That'll be Eoin's head hitting the *Beetle*'s roof,' Lally whispered to Gilles with a giggle. 'He always does that when he goes up on the bridge.'

The stage lights went off, leaving a single beam in the centre. Everyone leaned forward eagerly. Lally held her breath. Ever since that night she'd tried to knock on his door, she'd started paying more attention to what her dad was up to. In the past two weeks, while Eoin had been working on that puppet, she'd never caught sight of it. She'd barely caught sight of him either. He'd hardly left his cabin, coming out to eat or walk at odd times of the day and night. Just now, when he'd looked up at her on the bridge, she'd noticed that his skin, normally so brown from the outdoor life they lived, seemed pasty and his eyes looked bleary.

The scarf-wrapped shape dropped towards the stage.

'Ta-da!' Eoin said, as the scarf slipped away and the new puppet stood in the spotlight and opened up her arms in a salute.

Lally gasped. Beside her Gilles went still. A variety of 'ohs' and 'ahhs' broke out behind them.

The puppet was lovely. Her hair fell ebony black about her long thin body. She was dressed in dark green silk which fell in wispy folds about her legs. Her hands, legs and feet were reddish-brown, the natural shade of the hawthorn wood, but her face was milk-white – not what Lally had expected at all. Eoin rarely painted his puppets, preferring to allow their wooden origins to show.

'Aoife,' he said. 'Second wife of Lir, God of the Sea.'

The puppet began to move, causing another outbreak of approving noises from her audience.

'I've never seen a puppet move so gracefully, Eoin,' Des said. 'You've outdone yourself.'

Aoife turned her head towards Des, fixed him with her dark eyes and bowed. Everyone laughed.

'Just one question, Eoin,' Carla said. 'How does she turn into a witch-of-the-air when Lir punishes her for what she has done to his children? Or do we need a whole other puppet for that?'

Before their eyes Aoife rose in the air. A pair of filmy black wings spread out behind her and her white face flew away to reveal the darker carved face beneath.

'A mask,' Gilles said. 'That's so cool!'

That face, thought Lally. That face. I've seen it before...

'Wow,' Nette said. 'That's one great puppet.'

I've seen it before, Lally thought again, frozen to her seat. When we got stuck. On that wood. It looks just like...

The woman in the water.

'Bravo!' Claudine began to clap and they all joined in.

But she'd imagined that, hadn't she? Lally swallowed hard. There was no woman in the water. There couldn't have been. She shook her head. This must be déjà vu or whatever you call it. My mind is playing tricks, she thought.

'OK! My turn,' Nette said, standing up. 'Show me how you did that, Eoin.'

The puppet turned to stare at Nette.

'Actually, Nette, it's really difficult to do,' Eoin's voice said as the he pulled the puppet towards him so that only her feet were visible. 'I'm intending to work her myself.'

Lally felt rather than saw the exchanged glances.

'You're going to operate this puppet, is that what you're saying?' Carla asked. 'You're going to work up on the bridge every show?'

'Yes.' Eoin appeared around the side of the stage with the puppet in his arms, hidden again under the scarf.

'And who's going to direct?'

'I thought you could continue what you've begun. If that's OK with you.'

Carla paused. 'I guess it is,' she said.

'Great! Now, if no one minds, I badly need to get some kip.' Eoin smiled. 'See you all bright and early tomorrow.' He nodded at them all and walked towards the stern, gingerly cradling the puppet and her strings, whistling as he went.

'Fun and games tomorrow then,' Nette remarked.

'What does she mean?' Gilles asked Lally.

'I mean, Gilles,' Nette said, 'that you're all going to have some adjusting to do. Eoin may be lean but he's tall, and working with a lanky-limbed body up there is going to take a bit of getting used to. Meanwhile, I am puppet-less, so I suppose that puts me on front of house duty.'

'Do you mind?' Claudine asked.

'Not really,' Nette said. 'Though I must admit I'd love to have a go of that puppet. I've never seen anything quite like her before.'

'She's amazing,' Gilles said. 'Isn't she, Lally?'

'Amazing.' Lally forced a smile.

But he must have seen something in her face. 'Are you OK?' he asked. 'Is something wrong?'

Would Gilles think she was nuts if she told him what she was really thinking? That she wished they'd never brought the tree trunk on board *Beetle*, that she wished the man who'd tried to nick it had got away with it?

That she'd seen the puppet's face before.

Yes, she told herself, he will think you're nuts. Like he'd thought the people they'd read about in Ireland who changed the route of a road just to avoid cutting down a single hawthorn tree were nuts. He'll laugh at you. And he'll be right. Get a grip, Lally McBride. Seriously, get a grip.

'I'm fine,' she said to him. 'Absolutely fine.'

28th May 1596

W *ah?*
My own snore has awoken me with a start. Where am I?

I remember, I remember. I'm inside Master Waller's work chamber. I have fallen asleep here in my hiding place despite knowing that was the one thing I absolutely must not do.

How long has it been? It was twilight when I stole in. Now it is dark.

Is he here?

I hold my breath.

He is, he is. I can hear the scratching of his quill.

Has he heard me? Has he?

He must not have, for he goes on writing. In the darkness under my old work desk I am creased up like a dog. One leg has gone to sleep. I long to stretch it out and rub it back to life but I dare not. I let my breath out slowly, softly, and wait for my eyes to grow accustomed to the darkness. Master Waller will have candles lit but their light does not reach under here.

This evening at supper I complained of a headache and said I was going early to bed. Instead I crept in here, gaining entry using Annie's key, stolen from her in the afternoon. I am determined to know what Master Waller is doing. I need to know what causes the marks on his arms, the deep shadows under his eyes. I need to know why he locks himself in, why he locks me out.

At least, earlier today it all seemed vitally important. Right now I am at once racked with the fear of being discovered and so sleepy I can barely stifle my yawns.

What if the man is simply writing? Am I going to stay here all night listening to him run the quill across the page? How am I going to stay awake and avoid discovery?

But ... what is that strange smell?

I sniff the air silently. Earth, grass, sweet meadow flowers ... it's as if I was lying on my back in the high field out back of my family home in Chiswick.

What's that I hear? Two voices mumbling?

Is Master Waller speaking out the parts as he writes?

I listen harder.

My brain is still bleary with sleep but surely there are two voices intertwining?

One voice is his. The other has a woman's tone.

I am full awake now.

Yes. Two voices. A man's – my master's – and a woman's.

What can this mean?

Has Master Waller taken a mistress?

For there is no doubt there is a woman in the chamber

and now she is singing. I cannot make out the words of her song. Her voice sounds like a soft breeze rustling leaves. That too reminds me of home, but still I shiver.

The chamber was empty when I first arrived. She must have entered with Master Waller. He must sneak her up at night and out again before daylight. Till then I have no choice but to sit here quietly and see and hear things that are none of my business to see and hear.

Curse my curiosity! Bennet warned me not to meddle. Now here I am playing the peeper because I imagined something terrible and unnatural afoot. All the whyle 'tis but love!

My face is grown scarlet; I can feel it burn. Here, in the dark, where not a soul can see me, I am mortified by my own foolishness. If I escape undiscovered I swear I will never meddle in the doings of others again. Please God, please God, get me out of here without my master knowing I have spied on him and I will never do such a thing again. Never.

My wild imaginings about what ailed Master Waller are done away! The truth is so commonplace! A mistress!

I admit I am somewhat disappointed in him; he writes of love as such a pure and sacred thing, his women are all angels, virtuous and heroic, yet here he is engaged in night trysts of the most ordinary and base kind. The ridiculousness of it all is not lost on me; it bubbles in my throat and threatens to burst forth from me in hysterical laughter! I pinch myself good and hard.

Stay still, stay silent, stay awake!

I ease myself into a more comfortable position and order my heart to beat more quietly.

'Tis then I become aware that what light my eyes see is of a greenish hue. I become aware that the song I hear, for all its softness, is quivering through my very bones. The smell that first seemed sweet to my nostrils is now awakening memories of moulds, moths, and festering decay.

I have to look.

Just once.

I know I shouldn't. I have done Master Waller a deep wrong by being here; I should pry no further into his business. But I can't help it; I'm compelled to see the singer of this eerie song.

Gingerly, I uncurl my body and push it into an upright position. I grasp the table legs and slowly squeeze myself forward between them and the stool till my face is almost out in the light.

Master Waller is sitting at his desk. His pen flies across the paper; several full sheets litter the floor in front of me. Behind the playwright is a woman. She's beautiful. Her long arms curl about my master's as he writes. She sings and whispers in his ear. She rubs her cheek against his. She is almost naked but for a gauzy shift. I lower my gaze and begin to retreat into my hiding hole.

Wait! Something is amiss. Look again.

God's bread!

In the candlelight I can see Master Waller's eyes are glazed, his skin is slick with sweat. Not just the candle light illuminates him; light comes from the woman. Green light flickers and hovers about her skin like a phantasmal aura. Her long hair floats about her head as if she is submerged in water.

My master is not sitting; he is suspended by the woman, held up by her arms. His feet are not even in contact with the floor. I see the hawthorne trunk beneath him. She comes from it. That which should be her legs is submerged within its black twisted shape.

I think I may get sick. My mouth is suddenly dry as a year-dead hedgehog.

As I watch, the woman's hands uncurl, and long, skinny, twig-like fingers stretch and flex. They stroke Master Waller's arms gently, once, twice, thrice; then, to my horror, they pierce his skin, sinking into his veins like starved leeches.

I want to call out but my hands fly to my lips to stop my mouth. My limbs seize up with terror. I can feel my eyes popping in my head.

The wicked creature is feeding off him! I can see his life force pulsing through her fingers. Her light grows stronger; he grows paler. And yet he writes on like a madman as she sings her strange words in his ears.

What sorcery is this? What will I do? What can I do?

I want to crawl back in my corner, cover my head. Why did I come here? Why did I come here? Why do I have to bear witness to this – this – hideous exchange?

Make it stop, please God, make it stop.

But I am here. And it is not ceasing. She feeds on him; he writes. I am witness. I am the only one who can intervene.

Act, Flea! Gather your wits and act. You hid yourself to see what ailed your master. Now you are obliged to do something.

Save your master!

I draw a ragged half-breath.

'Stop!' I splutter, stumbling out of my hiding place.

I slip on the pieces of paper strewn about the floor, lose my footing and go sprawling face-down. Master Waller doesn't even turn his head, doesn't seem aware I'm here.

But she, she turns her lovely face.

Oh God! Her eyes are like two sloe berries, black and opaque. And they are fixed on me. I squirm on the floor, trying to find my feet, but I'm so petrified all I can manage is to crawl a small way backwards on my belly.

She hisses like an outraged cat and abruptly withdraws her fingers from Master Waller's arms. Her startled anger fills the chamber; her sweet song turns sharp and high. It becomes a shrill scream which judders through me, robbing me of what few wits I still possess. She grows upwards, towering over me, raising those awful hands above her, ready to pounce. I curl up frantically. I slap my hands over my eyes so as not to see her, then open my fingers to slits so I can. I hear myself whimpering.

I wish I was a hedgehog. I wish I was a flea on a hedgehog.

I cover my head with my arms, cower helplessly and wait for her attack.

FOURTEEN

'Right. I propose one more run-through from start to finish today.' Carla shushed the outbreak of groans backstage. 'And then a whole day off tomorrow. How's that sound?'

On the bridge Gilles turned to Lally and grinned. She rolled her eyes and mimed sleep. The last week of rehearsals had been intense and everyone was exhausted. Only Eoin looked unhappy with Carla's announcement.

'I'm not sure we can afford to take a day out, Carla,' he began. 'The show opens in five days and—'

'Overruled!' Carla's voice came from just beneath them; her face appeared under the stage opening. 'Sorry, Eoin. I'm putting my director's foot down this time. We'll all be the better for a day away from the puppets.'

Lally watched Eoin's face from behind her hair. He and Carla had been clashing a lot over the play. Carla thought it needed more lightness; Eoin wanted everything just as he had written it. At first their disagreements had been fairly good-humoured and Carla joked that she'd never had Eoin pegged for a control freak. 'There's only room for one of those on board,' she'd said, 'and I'm it.'

But they'd all got used to 'taking five' whenever Carla suggested a change to the script and Eoin disagreed. Somewhere along the way all the laughter and chat had gone out of rehearsals.

Right around the time Eoin had joined them on the bridge, Lally thought. Around the time the hawthorn puppet had been unveiled.

Lally couldn't remember this level of tension on any other show.

Maybe it's always like this near first night and I just never noticed, she reasoned, trying to push away thoughts of unlucky wood and death and lost limbs.

Eoin was scratching at his arm through his long-sleeved t-shirt. He'd been doing it all day, first one arm then the other. And yesterday, now that Lally thought about it. He was frowning; he was doing that a lot these days too. For a moment he looked as though he was going to argue with Carla again.

'Boat needs a pump-out,' Des said from behind them. 'We can't have the head getting blocked just as the shows start. And we're getting short of water. You and me can go get that sorted tomorrow, Eoin.'

Eoin's frown didn't lift but he nodded. Pumping out had to be done at the Old Canal Offices and took time, as did refilling the *Beetle*'s water tank.

'Fine, a day off it is then.' He gave a half-smile and Carla nodded and withdrew her head. 'Des and me will head off with the barge at nine o'clock; anyone who wants to spend the day elsewhere needs to be up and out by then.'

'Aye, aye, Captain,' Nette's voice came from below where she was changing scenery. She clacked her heels.

Everyone laughed and began to shuffle back into starting positions.

'What's up with your arms, Eoin?' Lally asked as she passed him.

'Nothing,' he snapped. 'Nothing's wrong.'

'But you're tearing at them every five minutes!' She reached over with her free right hand to tug his sleeve upwards.

'Hey!' he said and pulled his arm away quickly, but not quickly enough to stop her catching a glimpse of red raw skin and what looked like puncture marks.

'What are they?' Lally asked.

'What? These scratches? Carving wounds,' he said. 'Must have taken near as many lumps out of myself as I did herself.' He nodded to the puppet dangling beneath them.

'And they haven't healed yet?' Lally said. 'Eoin!'

'They're fine, don't fuss.' He smiled but there was impatience in his voice.

'They must be infected.' She touched his arm again. He pulled away sharply, so sharply Lally lost her balance and thwacked her hip against the leaning rail. He made to grab her with his left hand but she had already righted herself.

'Sorry, love,' he said, staring at her for a few seconds

as if he'd only just realised she was there. 'I didn't mean to … I guess Carla's right – we all need a break.' He turned away and bent forwards over the rail, arranged his fingers on the control and stared down the strings at his puppet below him.

'Music! Let's start,' Carla called.

Lally quickly switched her swan for the girl puppet.

'Maman wants to know if you'll spend the day with us tomorrow,' Gilles whispered as the opening phrases of music began.

Lally nodded. 'Sure,' she whispered. She tried to say 'that'd be lovely, thank you,' but her lip was trembling, so she gave Gilles a quick smile and leaned over the support to concentrate on the puppets.

Eoin had never snapped at her like that before. She'd sometimes heard him be slightly brusque with Des or Carla or Nette, but never with her. She bit down on her lip to stop it wobbling. I'm not a little girl any more, she thought. I have to get used to being treated like everyone else. And he's tired. Everyone's tired.

She glanced sideways at him. He was totally engrossed in his puppet, his long fingers expertly manoeuvring the strings. She could see his eyes had dark blots beneath them and that frown seemed to have set into his face permanently. Eoin's face, that usually broke so easily into a grin.

He had mentioned money several times lately. Were they in trouble? She knew the theatre ran on a shoestring, but maybe things were getting really tight?

Did that explain his uncharacteristic anxiety over this show, the grumpiness, and the rows with Carla? Why was he ignoring those sores on his arms and covering them with long-sleeved T-shirts in this warm weather?

She looked at the puppet he was working, the hawthorn puppet. She was wearing her white mask and her wings were folded out of sight behind her back. In a few moments Eoin would pull the strings that unfurled the wings and drew the mask away from her dark face. It was an amazing trick but it never failed to make Lally shiver.

FIFTEEN

L ally had never been on the tube before. Carla and
Nette had brought her to see some of London's
sights when she was little but they'd always taken the
bus – which made sense to her now she knew Carla
had problems with tunnels. This morning Claudine
had taken Lally and Gilles on the Bakerloo Line to
Waterloo where they found a nice French café for
breakfast.

'I propose our day out will be full of interesting
things which also count as educational,' Claudine
said as they sat down with coffees, hot chocolates
and croissants. 'It's still term time and when I pulled
Gilles out of school early I had to promise his teachers
this trip would be a very great learning experience for
him.'

Gilles groaned and Lally grinned as she smothered
her croissant in apricot jam.

'But first,' Claudine winked at Lally, 'we will go and
take a twirl on the London Eye!'

'Yes!' Gilles made a fist and punched the air.

After their 'twirl' on the Eye they walked along the
river past Waterloo Bridge and Gabriel's Wharf. As

they passed the Millennium Bridge a large thatched roof came into view, a roughly circular building with a roughly circular roof.

'That's where we are going,' Claudine said. 'The New Globe Theatre. Come on, hurry. The next tour starts soon.'

They bought their tickets in the foyer and joined a few other people in the basement of the building by a life-size model of an old oak tree. A young woman with a pierced eyebrow and a tattoo peeking from one sleeve approached them.

'You're for the tour?' she said jauntily. 'My name is Emmeline, I'll be your guide for the next forty minutes. Follow me.'

'Wow,' said Gilles as they entered the theatre itself. 'Just, wow.'

Lally knew what he meant. It was weird to think that this was how theatres had once looked. Big circular buildings open to the sky in the middle.

'It's like a partially covered amphitheatre,' Gilles said.

'Exactly,' said Emmeline. 'Or the bear pits, which were also very popular entertainments for the Tudors. Except instead of putting bears in the pit this is where most of the audience stood to watch the play.'

'Stood?' Lally said in astonishment.

'Yep. Just like most people will stand at a music concert. If you were wealthy enough you sat in the seats in the galleries, out of the rain and weather, and if you were very rich you might pay for a whole box just overlooking the stage.

'It's as exact a replica of the original Tudor Globe Theatre as we can make it,' she went on. 'The Globe of Shakespeare's time was built in 1599.'

She began to go into detail then, about the stage and the plays and how the New Globe itself came to be built. Lally only heard some of it; she was staring around her at the building, at the balconies, at the painted skies on the canopy above the stage. It was so big. She heard Emmeline say they could seat three thousand people in the original Globe. Three thousand! She couldn't even imagine that many people in one place. They could only seat fifty-five in the *Beetle*.

When the tour finished they watched Emmeline and another woman dress a male actor up as Shakespeare's Juliet.

'Because women were not allowed on stage then, all the female roles were performed by young men,' Emmeline said.

After they'd put on the various layers of clothing Tudor women wore, they made up the actor's face as it would have been for the stage.

'We can't use exactly what they used because the white make-up from Tudor times contained a lot of lead,' Emmeline explained. 'It's very likely the boys who played these parts day after day suffered from bad skin and stomach problems, both symptoms of lead poisoning. Many of them will have died young, poor things.'

In another corner two young women were being trained in sword fighting for a duelling scene. Lally, Gilles and Claudine watched for a while then took a look around the exhibition.

Back out on the street they found a nearby chip shop and walked to the riverside with their bags of fish and chips. The sun was shining and it felt like the whole city had come out to have lunch along the Thames. Neat shiny people in suits sat on the neat shiny terraces drinking lattes and eating salads and plates of food arranged in little towers.

'We are the – how do you say it – plebs?' Claudine laughed. 'Dressed down, eating out of paper.'

Lally nodded and glanced at their reflections in a shiny black marble wall. Gilles was wearing his usual skinny jeans and T-shirt. His hair had grown a bit since he'd first arrived. Claudine, despite her words, looked chic in black trousers and a grey shirt pulled in at the waist with a belt.

They don't look like plebs, she thought. They look … French.

Standing beside them she looked … scruffy. There was no full-length mirror on the *Beetle* and she hadn't noticed that her favourite hoodie looked two sizes too small for her. And her curly hair was especially out of control.

'It's going to rain,' she said.

Carla and Gilles looked at her and up at the clear sky. Twin mouth shrugs expressed their confusion.

'My hair,' Lally said. 'When it gets this wild, it's a sure sign that it's going to rain.'

They laughed.

'Your hair is wonderful,' Claudine said. 'The Pre-Raphaelites would have loved you. Rossetti would have painted you, isn't this true, Gilles?'

He nodded and reached out a hand to tug one stray curl.

'Is art a subject you like, Lally?' Claudine said.

'Sure.'

'Is that what you'll do in college?'

Lally blinked. No one had ever mentioned college before and she'd never really thought about it.

'Or theatre, maybe?' Claudine suggested. 'English literature? Creative writing?'

'I could do creative writing in college?' Lally rolled the idea around in her mind. 'I'd like that.'

'What A levels would you need?'

'I - I don't know.'

'We can look it up on Gilles's iPad when we get back, if you like,' Claudine said softly.

Lally nodded.

Carla and Nette used to be quite strict about her home-schooling hours but in the last year or so they'd left it up to her. Was she going to take GCSEs? What about her A levels? Why hadn't Carla or Eoin or Nette ever talked to her about college? She felt a sudden rising panic in her belly, then Claudine's hand closed gently on hers.

141

'You have plenty of time to think of the future, Lally,' she said. 'Have you ever been to France?'

'No, I've never been away from the *Beetle*.'

'You should come to Paris for a bit,' Claudine said. 'You could come back with us, attend school with Gilles for a term. It would help you with your French.'

'That would be cool,' Gilles said, turning his head to grin at her.

It would be more than cool, it would be brilliant! It would be the most fantastic thing ever. Lally grinned back at him, her eyes sparkling with excitement.

'OK. One more stop before we go back to the barge.' Claudine stared at her map of London. 'The New Globe was fascinating but it was a replica. I want to see the real thing, a real Tudor theatre. And there is one that way, I think.' She pointed down a side street.

'This was a theatre?' Gilles asked.

They were standing in a space which appeared to be the basement of a modern multi-storey apartment block. Lally leaned against the railings and peered through the darkness at a large murky puddle outlined by fluorescent tube lighting.

The caretaker who had let them in laughed. 'I know it doesn't look like much now, but yes, you are looking at what remains of the Rose Theatre. It was discovered in 1989. The tube lighting follows the outlines of the original footprint and the excavations have to be kept wet to protect them until money is found to preserve them permanently – hence the puddle. There's information about it on the walls behind you.' He wandered back out to his desk at the entrance.

'Imagine,' Claudine said. 'Shakespeare stood here. I mean, he really stood here. Some of his plays were performed right here. This is as close as we can ever get to breathing the air he breathed.'

Gilles laughed but Lally felt goosebumps break out along her arms. Maybe it was the cool air in this dimly lit space but she didn't think so.

'I didn't know this existed,' she whispered to Claudine. 'I didn't know. It's amazing.' She turned around in a circle to take it all in. '"Romeo, Romeo, wherefore art thou, Romeo?"' she said suddenly, leaning over the railing and throwing her arms out.

'"To be or not to be, that is the question,"' said Gilles, striking a pose.

'"Love is blind, and lovers cannot see the pretty follies that themselves commit,"' said Claudine.

'"Friends, Romans, countrymen, lend me your ears."'

'"Neither a borrower nor a lender be."'

'"To thine own self be true."'

'"A rose by any other name would smell as sweet."'

'"To be or not to be, that is the question."'

'You said that one already,' Lally said, poking Gilles in the ribs.

'I can't think of any more. I was hoping no one would notice.' He shrugged and grinned.

For a few minutes they were all silent, standing together staring at the outline glowing in the water.

The theatre, Lally thought. It's in my blood, it's part of me. I'd like to work in the theatre. Write plays, maybe. Or direct them.

She felt a sudden surge of excitement, knowing something had planted itself in her head, something all her own. Something she could think about and figure out for herself.

'It's closing time,' the caretaker said from the doorway.

Claudine took one more look at the puddle. 'This is very special,' she said. 'To be standing here.'

'Yes,' Lally said. 'It is.'

'Hope you have umbrellas,' said the caretaker as they made their way to the exit. 'It's chucking it down out there, cats and dogs.'

SIXTEEN

A jackdaw was sitting on the *Beetle*'s roof when they got back, scrunched up in a belligerent black hump beside the chimney. It didn't move when Gilles flapped his hands at it.

Crow. The thought jumped into Lally's head before she could push it away. Jackdaws are a type of crow. Animal familiars of hawthorn witches.

'Stupid bird,' Gilles said. 'Go to the trees. It's wet out here.'

It rolled its blue eyes away. They laughed and piled through the door, down the steps into the chow house.

'I can't wait to get out of these clothes.' Lally pulled the wet denim away from her skin and kicked off her squelchy shoes.

Claudine wrinkled her nose and nodded. 'Dry clothes, dry hair and a mug of coffee,' she said. 'In that order.'

'Is that music coming from the theatre?' Gilles asked. 'What is it? It's not from the show.'

They all stood, listening. Through the drum of rain on the roof a tin whistle was mournfully calling. Lally followed it down the passageway and the others came after her, all of them unconsciously staying silent. In the theatre all was dim. On the stage the girl swan was swimming alone on the waves. The scenery was set to the backdrop for the second lake on which the swan children were doomed to spend three hundred years; the lake of storms. The swan was hanging her head sadly.

Lally recognised the tune that was playing. It was called 'The Lonesome Boatman'. She'd often heard Des whistle it when he was standing at the *Beetle*'s tiller. She slipped into the front row to watch and Claudine and Gilles slid in beside her.

A shadow crept over the weeping swan. The witch-of-the-air was hovering above the lake. The swan child turned her head, saw her stepmother and recoiled. The music quickened slightly but the witch opened her arms to the swan in a gesture of pity.

God, that puppet gave her the creeps. Was this some sort of new scene? Was the witch regretting what she had done?

Yes, it seemed she was. She flew down towards the swan, who flared her wings and pulled back her head the way swans do when they are signalling anger. The witch bowed and again reached her upturned palms towards her stepchild. The swan darted her beak towards the witch as if to strike her then turned away in sorrow. The witch leaned towards the swan, her drooping head echoing the girl's. The music swirled around the stage again. The swan child drew her long neck in an arc and spread her white wings; the witch spread her black wings and raised her arms to the sky. The swan rose up from the water, joined the witch amongst the storm clouds and they began a sort of flying dance.

It was beautiful. The puppetry was controlled and precise, every lovely little gesture of wing and head and hand clearly speaking the emotions of the characters. But Lally shivered. It didn't matter how many times she told herself the hawthorn stuff she had read was nonsense; the witch puppet made her skin crawl.

At first the swan child was angry, resisting the remorseful pleadings of the witch. As her stepmother continued to beg forgiveness, however, she softened and they danced together, the white wings and the black beating in time, mirroring each other's movements as the music became more urgent.

They share a similar fate, Lally thought. That's what the dance means. The girl and her brothers must forever live as swans upon the lakes; the witch is doomed to stay forever airborne. The stepmother's curse has rebounded on her and trapped her as surely as she trapped the children of Lir.

'Enough,' a voice said. The swan girl suddenly went slack and the music stopped abruptly. 'I get it, it's really lovely but it's going to make the show too long.'

Carla. Carla was on the bridge operating the swan. Lally cleared her throat to say hello.

'We'll cut the Bear and Wolf scene from Act Two.' Eoin's voice.

'What? It's the only bit of humour there is in the entire show.'

'But it's not true to the original legend.' Eoin was speaking quickly, as if he'd drunk too much coffee. 'I put it in to soften the story a bit but now I think we should take it out. It doesn't belong.'

'Having the stepmother turn up to beg forgiveness in the second half of the show isn't authentic either, is it?'

'No. But it works and it allows us to use her again. She's what this show is all about.'

'I thought it was about the swan children.' Lally heard Carla take a deep breath. When she spoke again it was in the same even, patient tone she'd been using all along. 'It doesn't matter. This show needs some lightness, Eoin. We can't take out Bear and Wolf.'

'But—'

'And we are not putting in another dark scene. Our audience is mainly children, for heaven's sakes.'

'I'm not asking your permission, Carla.' Eoin sounded like he was talking through gritted teeth.

On the stage Lally saw the witch puppet twitch.

'I thought I was the director?' Carla said quietly.

'It's my play.'

His sharp tone made Lally flinch. Please, not another argument, she thought. Why is he always picking rows these days?

'You wrote it but we all make it happen; you know that.' Carla's voice was growing concerned. 'What's up with you, Eoin? I've never seen you like this. You don't look well. Is something wrong?'

'Nothing's wrong with *me*.' The emphasis came down so hard on 'me' that Lally squirmed in her seat.

'What do you mean by that, exactly?' Carla's voice rose.

'Any fool can see this scene should go in,' Eoin said, his voice rising also. 'I don't care what age the audience is, this scene is in.'

'You're being unreasonable. We'll talk about this later with Nette and Des.'

The swan child floated into the air as if Carla was about to hook her onto one of the pipes. The witch puppet rose abruptly after her, her wings flaring wide. The two puppets touched, their strings and wings tangling in a blur of black and white. There was a sharp cry and suddenly the puppets were tumbling onto the stage. As they hit the boards in a clatter of small flailing limbs and wings, something large came crashing after them, landing on top of them with a sickening thud.

SEVENTEEN

'Carla!' Lally dashed forward to the stage. 'Carla!'

Carla lay quite still. Her body, half on stage and half off, was twisted. One arm was sticking out at a strange angle.

'Carla? Say something,' Lally said, reaching out to touch her.

'Don't!'

Lally looked up at Eoin towering above them on the bridge. His hands were gripping the leaning rail so tight his knuckles were white.

'Don't move her,' he said urgently. 'Is she breathing?'

Lally leaned closer and peered into Carla's face. Her eyes were closed but Lally could hear small rasps coming from her slightly parted lips.

'Yes,' she said. Her voice came out in a jagged whisper.

This couldn't be happening. Carla couldn't be lying there on the stage like a broken doll. Only a moment ago she'd been talking. Only a moment ago everything had been fine. Well, except that she and Eoin had been arguing.

Lally looked back at her father. His face was lost

somewhere between the shadows and the glare of the stage lights. 'What happened?'

Eoin shook his head impatiently. 'Go get Nette and Des. Is Gilles there? Tell him to ring for an ambulance. Move, Lally.'

'I'll get Nette.' Claudine's voice was so close to Lally it made her jump. Gilles got his phone out of his pocket as his mother disappeared towards the stern.

'112?' he asked.

'Or 999,' Lally said. She turned back towards Carla and reached her hand towards her again, meaning to stroke her hair.

'No!' Eoin had climbed down the ladder and was leaning in towards Carla with scissors in his hand. 'I mean ... hold on a second while I cut her free of the puppets. The ambulance people won't need that complication.' He gave Lally a tight smile and she moved out of his way as he began to cut the strings which had somehow closed about Carla like a spider web. He gingerly slid the swan girl out from under Carla's left leg and handed it to Lally. It was in a sorry state, one wing smashed and its neck twisted.

Like Carla, Lally thought, trying to choke back a sob.

Eoin went to work on the witch puppet.

Did he really need to be so careful and slow? Was it Carla he was trying not to hurt or that wretched puppet? The idea flickered through Lally's mind but she pushed it away. He was being careful in case Carla had a neck or back injury. And the argument they were having – that had nothing to do with Carla falling. It couldn't have.

The witch puppet came out all in one piece. Even her filmy wings seemed undamaged. Eoin pushed her away into the far corner, out of reach. He laid a hand on Carla's head and leaned into her.

'I'm sorry, Carla,' Lally heard him whisper. 'I'm so sorry.' There was a catch in his voice.

How had she fallen? Lally wanted to know so badly, but she couldn't bring the words to her mouth. How did she fall off the bridge when there was a support to protect her?

'What happened?' Nette came rushing in and pushed past Lally and Gilles. 'Is an ambulance coming?'

Gilles nodded.

Nette leaned in beside Carla and took hold of her free hand.

'What happened, Eoin? How did she fall?'

'I–I'm not sure.' He moved off the stage to give Nette more room. 'We'd just finished trying out a new scene when she went to hang up her puppet. Next thing, she yelled and yanked her hand away from the strings, as though something had hurt her. She lost her footing and came off the bridge. It was as if–' He hesitated and shook his head.

'As if what?'

'As if she'd received an electric shock.' He ran his hands through his hair. 'I wasn't quick enough to grab her. I'm sorry.'

Lally could see he was blinking back tears. She folded her arms tightly around her body and tried to hold in the sob lodged in her chest.

Wake up, Carla, she thought. Open your eyes and tell us you're all right.

But her arm wasn't all right. It had to be broken to be sticking out from under her body at such a strange angle. And she was so white.

Gilles's fingers touched Lally's shoulder lightly and she leaned back against him. 'Where's the ambulance?' she whispered. 'Why doesn't it come?'

'It will be here soon,' he said quietly. 'It's only been five minutes.'

When they arrived, the ambulance workers were fast and efficient. Carla was carefully manoeuvred onto a hand-held stretcher, slowly lifted up the stairs and down the gangplank. The narrowness and steepness of the steps up to the street caused difficulties but, after what seemed like forever, Carla was placed in the ambulance. Nette was going with them to the hospital.

'Come with me, Lally,' Nette said suddenly and grabbed Lally's arm. Lally nodded and one of the ambulance men helped her in beside Nette. As the doors closed Lally looked out through glass. Claudine, Des and Gilles were in a tight huddle. Eoin was standing apart.

He looks as upset as everyone else, Lally thought. This was an accident. Nothing to do with Eoin and nothing to do with that stupid hawthorn puppet.

But even before the ambulance began to move she saw his eyes glaze over. And as the siren began to wail and they pulled out onto the road, Lally watched his gaze stray to the theatre barge down below. He flexed his fingers. A familiar gesture, one all puppeteers were inclined to. A movement made in preparation just before taking up the strings.

EIGHTEEN

'She's conscious? That's great news.' Des looked up from the mobile phone and gave everyone at the breakfast table the thumbs-up. 'What? She's not making much sense? But that's normal, right?'

At the table all the spoons of cereal stayed suspended in mid-air. Lally held her breath. What was normal? What?

'To be expected. OK. And her arm? Right, uh-huh. Arm's broken in two places,' he said. 'Mm-hm. She'll have to wear a collar? Right. But her back is OK? Bruised. Right, sure, sure. Bye.'

He put the phone down on the table. 'You got most of that?'

Everyone nodded, stunned.

'No,' said Lally. 'Say it again, please.'

'Basically she's fine,' Des said, with a tired smile. 'A bit dazed, not saying much, doesn't remember falling. Her back is grand but she'll have to wear a collar on her neck for a while. Her arm needs pins and a cast. They're going to do that today which means an operation, so Nette is staying put.' He reached out a hand and ruffled Lally's hair. 'Main thing is, she's going to be fine. OK?'

Lally nodded and bit her lip. She'd been so happy

when she'd arrived back at the barge yesterday with Claudine and Gilles, so full of the city and the theatre and her own ideas. Now Carla was in hospital and Lally wasn't even sure when she'd last had a proper conversation with her.

She and Nette had sat with Carla in Accident and Emergency for hours last night. In all that time Carla hadn't moved. Every now and then a nurse would come over and take her blood pressure, feel her pulse and shine a light in her eyes. Lally had never been so scared in her life. Nette had sat clutching Carla's hand and talking to her quietly.

The hospital staff were lovely but couldn't tell them very much, other than that they'd know more when Carla woke up and could answer questions. Des and Eoin had arrived later to see how things were going and to bring Lally back to the *Beetle*. She'd been exhausted when they'd reached the boat but had hardly slept for worrying.

And now Carla needed a neck collar and an operation. Pins and a cast. That didn't sound so OK, fine, normal. That sounded pretty awful.

'First performance of *The Children of Lir* is this coming Tuesday as scheduled, unless Des has found something wrong with the electrics,' Eoin was saying now.

Des shook his head. 'I had a good look at the lights and wires above both bridges and there's nothing loose, out of place or broken that I could see. I've doubled up on the electrical tape, just to be safe, but I really don't think it was a shock that caused Carla to take that tumble.' Des took a slurp of black tea. 'How about you lot?' he said, looking at Claudine, Gilles and Lally. 'You were sitting out front, watching. What did you see?'

'The witch attacked the swan child and a giant fell down from the sky,' Claudine replied.

Des blinked. 'Excuse me?' he said.

'I don't mean to sound, ah, how do you say – flippant?' Claudine gave her usual mouth shrug and spread her hands out uncertainly. 'We were watching the puppets and we saw the illusion, not what actually happened. At least, that's how it was for me.' She turned to Gilles who nodded his agreement.

'Lally?' Des looked at her.

She replayed those moments in her mind. 'It's like Claudine says. Our eyes were on the puppets. The witch puppet spread her wings and got tangled up with the swan girl, then suddenly Carla was falling to the stage.'

And you were fighting with her, she wanted to say to Eoin. But she couldn't bring herself to; it would sound like an accusation.

'Also—' Claudine hesitated. 'Excuse me, Eoin, but we overheard you arguing with Carla before it happened. Not, I'm sure, that that had anything to do with it.'

'Eoin?' Des turned his head to where Eoin was standing, leaning against the galley counter, his face half in shadow.

'We were just discussing stuff. We had a difference of opinion, that's all.' Eoin shook his head. 'Myself and Carla haven't been seeing eye to eye much on this show. We'd agreed to let it rest for the time being. I was turning away when it happened. She yelled as though something had hurt her and then she fell. Like they described.' He straightened abruptly. 'The swan child is in a bit of a mess; are we going to be able to mend her?'

'Yes,' Claudine said. 'Gilles and I, we fixed her last night when you were all at the hospital.'

'Great.'Eoin put his mug down on the counter. 'Lally, you saw the new scene I wanted to put in; d'you think you're up for rehearsing that now?' he asked, stepping out of the galley into the light.

She ducked her head behind her hair so he couldn't see her eyes but she could see his. 'What about the scene with Bear and Wolf?'she asked quietly.

'We'll keep it. Carla wanted it left in. I want the new scene. We'll compromise by having them both.'

'Even if it makes the show too long?'

'So, it'll be too long.'

'OK.' She shook her hair away and tried to read his face. He looked anxious and drawn yet his focus was on the show when all she could think about was Carla.

'Right.' He rubbed his hands together. 'Rehearsals this morning as usual, then it's time for our first flyer hand-out.'

Des groaned.

'Flyer hand-out?' Gilles said.

'We'll be spending lunchtime outside cafes and tube

158

stops handing out flyers advertising the shows,' Lally explained. 'Then we'll post them in letterboxes in the afternoon.'

'It's time to let the locals know there's a show to come and see,' Eoin said. 'First night, here we come.'

NINETEEN

The curtain fell. On the stage the puppets went still; on the bridge everyone held their positions and waited. When the applause came it was loud and long. Lally heard Eoin let out a ragged breath. He slumped over the leaning rail as if he'd just finished a marathon.

'Someone needs to get out front quickly to help Des,' he said.

He flicked a switch and the house lights went up. Everyone jumped for the ladders at once. From the bridge the show had felt good, great even. It had just been Lally, Eoin, Gilles and Claudine up there since Des had to replace Nette on door and refreshments duty. Onstage Eoin and Lally had had to sort all the scenery and props as well as working extra puppets and scenes. Apart from a few first-night hiccups – Wolf's tail had dropped off unexpectedly mid-flick, and the waves had malfunctioned briefly in Scene Three – everything had flowed really well. But how had it seemed to the audience?

'Magic!' That was the word they heard most at the door.

'Haunting.'

'So sad, so beautiful.'

'The best show you've done.'

Some children asked to see the swan puppets up close and Lally went to ask Eoin. He lifted the hawthorn puppet off the stage and hung her behind him, out of sight. Then he nodded his head.

'I'll work the swans; can't let the kids see them lifeless. You stay out front and make sure no one makes a grab.'

At the chow house some families hung around and ordered more drinks and biscuits like it was interval time again. That had never happened before but Gilles and Claudine got the kettle going. No one was in a hurry to end the evening. Claudine grabbed some flyers and handed them to the adults.

'Tell your friends,' she said, beaming at them. 'Tell them to come.'

'Celebratory hot chocolates?' Claudine asked Gilles and Lally when at last the barge had emptied out.

Lally began to shovel some chocolate powder into some paper cups.

'Non! Special hot chocolates,' Claudine said, reaching into a cupboard and pulling out some packages. 'Real French chocolate.'

'Sounds good,' Eoin said, appearing from the theatre. 'Punters all gone?'

'Yes. Wasn't it fantastic?' Claudine's eyes were shining. 'You will have a hot chocolate, yes?'

'He will have a hot chocolate, no.' Des stopped in the act of unfolding the table and putting it out ready for breakfast. 'We are going for a pint, him and me. This man has hardly been off the barge in a month, unless you count the dash to hospital the other night. Speaking of which, I just took a call from Nette. She'll be bringing Carla home tomorrow.'

'That's terrific news.' Claudine patted Lally's arm.

'You lot enjoy your hot chocolates and we'll be back in an hour bearing five bags of chips.' Des handed Eoin his jacket. 'Come on. I'm not taking no for an answer.'

For a moment Eoin looked as if he might refuse. 'I'll just be a sec,' he said finally. 'I have to put – I need to go to my cabin first.'

He has to put that puppet away, Lally thought. In his room.

She hated that he kept her there. The puppet was creepy and the way Eoin kept her close all the time – that was creepy too. And now, as he left his cabin, she'd swear she heard him turn the key in the lock. She tipped back her chair to get a view of him as he came back into the chow house. He was slipping the key into his pocket.

He and Des left and Claudine handed Gilles and Lally the *Beetle*'s best mugs. Into the mugs she dropped a handful of chocolate drops, dark and milk mixed. She took the pan of milk off the heat and poured some over the chocolate. 'Stir,' she said. 'Then decorate.' She opened a bag of tiny white marshmallows and another of chocolate flakes.

'Your father is a workaholic, Lally,' she said. 'I didn't

realise this when we first came. I thought he was very – how do you say it? – laid back.'

'Eoin *is* laid back,' Lally said with a frown. 'Everyone always says that.' And everyone always did. Laid back, easy-going, chilled – that's what people said about her dad. She'd never heard anyone accuse him of being a workaholic before.

Claudine and Gilles pulled identical mouth shrugs. Gilles buried his face in his mug and Claudine gave Lally one of her brilliant smiles. 'It is not a criticism. He has a lot of responsibilities, no? This show has been a gamble, something different. He must have been worried it would fail. Then the accident on Friday. Most people would be stressed by these things. I suppose I am saying my first impression of him was that nothing would faze him when he is actually rather nervous, I think. It's funny how our first impressions about people can be mistakes, yes?'

'I suppose,' Lally said. What could she say? Claudine's first impression wasn't wrong, and yet her description of Eoin now, a month after she'd first met him, wasn't wrong either.

'He's very possessive of that puppet,' Claudine said. 'I would give anything to try her out but he hides her away, keeps her with him all the time.'

Lally saw Gilles elbow his mother and he switched the subject back to how well the show had gone. Lally let them chatter.

Why didn't the witch puppet hang onstage like the

rest of the puppets in the show? Why was Eoin so weird about her? He was acting weird about a lot of things. Something had to be wrong. She'd ask Nette and Carla about it when they got home.

Or maybe she should leave it alone. Maybe this was just her dad being a temperamental artist or something. The show had been fantastic, after all. She couldn't remember an audience being this excited, this responsive. It had been thrilling. She wished Carla and Nette had been here to see it, to be part of it.

She stirred her drink with one of the flakes. Right now she was going to enjoy this delicious hot chocolate. And Carla was coming home tomorrow.

Maybe whatever had been wrong was coming right again.

TWENTY

Nette had asked that everyone give Carla a little time to settle into the barge before calling round, so Lally had satisfied herself with a welcoming wave when they arrived back from the hospital at one o'clock. As soon as the matinee was over, though, and the audience had finally left the barge, she stepped off *Beetle* and knocked on one of *Bird*'s windows.

'Permission to come aboard?' she called.

'Come on down.'

All the barge windows were shut so Nette's reply was rather muffled. There was smoke coming from *Bird*'s chimney and a wave of heat hit Lally as she stepped into the wheelhouse.

'Carla's cold,' Nette explained as Lally came into the living space.

Carla was sitting on the settle, propped up on cushions and wrapped in a heavy blanket. With the neck collar and the cast on her arm she looked frail. Her hair was spread around her shoulders and for the first time Lally noticed how much the black was streaked with grey.

She looks old, Lally thought, as she gave Carla a

165

careful hug. Carla wrapped her free arm around her and pulled her close.

'I won't break,' Carla said, but her voice shook and her smile wobbled. 'Sit beside me, love, and tell me how you are.'

'I'm great,' said Lally. 'The show went brilliantly last night and today, too. Everyone's really excited. Maybe you could come and see it tonight.'

Carla shook her head and looked anxiously at Nette.

'No, she won't come yet, Lal, love.' Nette smiled and frowned at the same time. 'Maybe next week sometime.'

Carla shook her head again. 'It's too cold to go out,' she said suddenly. 'This winter weather is so harsh.'

Lally looked at Nette, startled. 'Winter? It's not winter, Carla—' she began, but Nette put a finger to her lips and beckoned Lally towards *Bird*'s galley area. Lally stood up and followed.

'She's still a bit confused,' Nette whispered. 'The doctors said it will pass. Anything about the show seems to upset her – they think it's because her memory of the actual fall hasn't come back yet, so it's uncomfortable somehow. Could you change the subject? Talk about something else?'

Lally thought for a moment. She'd been so caught up in the show recently. Paris! She'd forgotten about Paris.

She smiled brightly and turned back to Carla who was picking absently at one of the dots on her blanket.

'There's something I wanted to tell you. I've been

166

invited to go to Paris,' Lally said. 'Claudine says I can go back with her and Gilles and she'll enrol me for a term in Gilles's school. Wouldn't that be amazing? Do you think I'll be able to go?'

'Go!' Carla said, brightening. 'Go, Lally.' She grabbed Lally's hand. 'Go to Paris!'

'No!' Nette said the word sharply. 'Lally can't go to Paris, Carla, you know that.' She gave Carla a queer look and Carla frowned and went back to studying the pattern on the blanket.

Lally felt her heart drop. 'Why can't I go?' she asked.

'Money,' Nette said. 'There won't be enough money to cover a trip like that.'

'But I've only got really basic French, Nette,' Lally said. 'How am I going to get my GCSE with only a few words?'

'Your GCSE? You don't have to take GCSEs.' Nette sounded slightly flustered. She kept looking at Carla to back her up, but Carla was rubbing Lally's hand, her expression as disappointed as Lally's.

'Why wouldn't I take them?' Lally's voice faltered.

'Home-schoolers don't have to. You have to do your A levels when you're eighteen but that's years away. You only do four subjects for your As and you surely don't intend taking a foreign language, do you?'

'I don't know – maybe. But either way, I'd like to speak French. You and Carla always say education should be about acquiring knowledge for knowledge's sake, not about exams.'

Nette blinked. 'Well, if Carla's arm takes a while to heal – and they said it could take ages – we won't be able to put on a show without you, so you'll be needed here come September. Please stop talking about it now, you're upsetting Carla,' Nette declared in a voice that said 'that's the end of that'. She turned away and began to wash some dishes in the sink, clanking them about and running both taps as if the onboard water supply was endless.

But that's not fair, Lally thought, shocked. She wanted to blurt it out, shout it even. And why was Nette so against her going to Paris? She wished she'd asked Eoin about it first but he was being so distant he'd probably have dismissed it out of hand as well. Why were all the adults in her life acting so strangely this summer? Lally had thought she was the one who was changing but now it seemed everyone else was. She looked at Carla, sitting beside her swathed in blankets on a summer's day, her eyes unfocused. She looked at Nette's back, uncharacteristically rigid and forbidding.

'That's not fair, Nette.' Lally almost whispered the words.

The woman at the sink stopped her noise. Her shoulders sank and she turned off the taps.

'I'm sorry, Lal,' she said, without turning. 'It's been a bad couple of days. I just can't think about this now. But you're right.' She turned and half-smiled. 'That wasn't fair.'

Lally nodded. 'I'd better go,' she said, standing up.

'Sure,' Nette said, drying her hands on her jeans. 'I'll see you to the door.' She moved ahead of Lally towards the stern.

'Lal!' Carla caught Lally's hand again and stared into her face. 'Don't mind what Nette says. You must do it.'

'My GCSEs?' Lally said, startled by Carla's sudden vehemence.

'Go to – wherever you said.'

'Paris?'

'Yes. There. Go. Go, get away from here. Get away from her.'

'Who? Nette?' Lally blinked. The way Carla looked, the way she was behaving – it was frightening her. Everything had been fine just last week. Just last month. Before…

'No. Her.' Carla looked back towards *Bird*'s wheelhouse. Lally followed her gaze through the windows to where *Ladybird*'s stern almost touched *Beetle*'s.

'The *Beetle*? Get away from *Beetle*?'

Carla's grip on her hand slackened and when she looked at Lally, she seemed confused. 'Yes,' she said at last. 'Get away from her.'

The 11th day of June, in the year of our Lord, 1596

I still have nightmares. Every night I wake up ready to scream aloud. It's her. She's coming for me, her talons descending ... I bite my tongue and force myself to stay still and wait for the fear to pass.

This is not Master Waller's house, I remind myself. Shhh! Calm down. You're far away, in another house, on the other side of the Thames. Do not wake Christopher and John.

I look at the two small boys sleeping beside me in the bed. I mustn't disturb them with my nightmares. I do not want them running next door to their father, my new master, with tales of my unquiet sleep.

Every night it's the same. I go to bed, praying for peaceful slumber, and every night I'm visited by horrible visions of what happened in Master Waller's work chamber. Every night I wake, sweating and trembling and remembering the awfulness of it and the humiliation that followed.

Bennet and Tom and Nashe and Hobbes proved false friends. Certainly, they all came stumbing up the stairs that night on hearing my screams, but by then Master

170

Waller had come to his senses and bundled me out of his chamber.

My legs wobbled so I couldn't support myself and my teeth were rattling fit to dash each other to pieces. I slid down the wall and lay in a quivering heap.

'Go, go look,' I jabbered, pointing a shaking finger towards the door. 'Go look and see the horrid thing that dwells within.'

Bennet – I'll give him his due – only hesitated a moment before pushing Master Waller aside, flinging open the door and entering, closely followed by Hobbes. But they were out again in a trice.

'There's no one there, Flea,' Bennet said through gritted teeth. 'What is it you think you've seen?'

'A creature, a-a sprite, some m-monster of the h-hawthorne trunk,' I stammered. 'I s-said no good would come from bringing it within the house.'

Bennet jerked his head at Hobbes who went back in and fetched the aforesaid thing out and placed it down between us all. Only I observed Master Waller flinch when Bennet kicked it roughly.

'It's a piece of wood, you dotard!' Bennet roared. 'A piece of dead wood!'

I tried to tell them what had happened but I was so undone I could only gibber: 'Black eyes, her eyes were black ... her hair floated about her head ... his arms, make him show you his arms ... they are covered in her marks where the twigs go in...'

I did something foolish then; I snatched at Master

Waller's wrist. His eyes flew wide open in rage. Before I knew it he'd grabbed my hand and twisted it behind my back, pushed me down the stairwell, beaten me across the hall, opened the door and thrown me out onto the street. The actors followed after and stood slack-mouthed while Master Waller called me a liar and a knave and ordered that I be not let inside his house again. The door was closed on me and remained closed to me, though I beat on it a full half hour.

I hung about the street for what remained of that night, and for all the next day, convinced that I must save Master Waller from himself, that someone must listen to me, someone must believe.

But Master Waller stayed within the house, and Annie too. The actors avoided me or shook me off when I approached them on their way to rehearsals at the Rose. They never spoke a word but their eyes called me mad, named me pitiful. Nevertheless, I kept my vigil over the house from a doorway opposite, despite the dirt, the tossed chamber pots, and all the dangers of the street. Not that a cutpurse or a foist would have wasted his knife or cuttlebung on me – I had no purse upon my belt to steal, my shirt was torn from the rough handling Master Waller had dealt me, and I was filthy from a run-in with a drift of hogs.

On the second night Tom sneaked out to me. He hustled me a small ways up the street and glanced back at the house.

'Your belongings,' he hissed, thrusting a bundle at

172

me and a loaf of bread. 'Annie sent the loaf. Bennet said, for pity's sakes, give up your crazed imaginings and go and find yourself a new position. To this end I am to give you my second-best shirt and bid you clean yourself and go tomorrow to the hirings at *Saint Paul's Cathedral.'*

I began to protest, to insist I'd witnessed what I'd said I had, but rather spoiled my point by stuffing my mouth with Annie's loaf as I spoke, for I was ravenous. Tom shook his head sadly at me and rubbed my hair.

'You are a daft coney, Flea,' he said. 'What craziness you talk! You must be away by first light tomorrow; the master has ordered Hobbes and Nashe to drive you off if you're still here and to set the law on you if you return. I'd let you indoors to sleep the night within the hall but we are all warned, on pain of our employment, to have nothing to do with you. Here, Hobbes sent you this—' he took half a lark and pigeon pie out of his shirt '—and Nashe sent you that.' He pressed a coin into my hand, looking around for any watchers in the shadows.

He wished me luck and left me to the darkness and cold pie. Cold pie, a loaf, a shirt, a coin – were they not kind gifts from concerned friends? At first I tried to convince myself they were, but as those long, dark, sleepless hours wore on, I understood. They were given to me in guilt and pity. They were given to me to bribe me into quiet acquiescence.

Go away, Flea, you are an embarrassment. Creep away, Flea, you crazy coney.

Hot, angry tears fell down my face as I finished the loaf and began to devour the pie.

I had been a true servant to Master Waller.

I had.

And, despite their scorn, I'd tried to warn the actors of what was in the house. I could leave with a clear conscience.

At dawn next morning I went to the edge of the river and bathed myself, as Bennet had ordered, wiped the snot and tears off my face and changed into Tom's second-best shirt.

'Master Waller's well-being is not my concern,' I said aloud to some gulls and a moorhen as I brushed dust and dirt off my breeches and dragged my comb through my hair. 'I did my best to help him. He has dealt ill with me and I owe him and his household nothing more.'

The gulls ignored me and the moorhen paddled away. I settled my hat upon my head and made my way over London Bridge.

TWENTY-ONE

'Phew! The bridge was like an oven today,' Gilles said, lying on *Beetle*'s roof with his legs hanging over the side.

Lally was stretched out beside him. A cool breeze was blowing off the water and it felt good after two hours backstage.

'I need a shower,' Gilles said.

'I know you do!' Lally laughed and dodged a sideswipe. 'But it's not your turn for a shower today, you're tomorrow.'

'Swap?'

'Nope! I'm looking forward to it too much.' Lally sat up on her elbows. 'This roof is hot too. It's been a really warm day.'

'And we work in a tin can with a rationed water supply.'

'Don't call *Beetle* a tin can, you'll hurt her feelings.'

Gilles snorted.

'It's funny...' Lally hesitated. 'Carla said I should go, get away from *Beetle*. Don't you think that was a strange thing to say?'

'When you asked about Paris, you mean? I thought they said you couldn't go?'

'Nette did. It was all a bit weird. Everyone's acting weird. Except Des.'

'Adults *are* weird,' Gilles said.

'They weren't always weird though. Eoin and Nette, I mean. And Carla's had a head injury, so it's not her fault.'

'But she's getting better, yes?'

'I don't know. Nette says so but she keeps making excuses for why I shouldn't visit. She says Carla is sleeping or it's not a good time, or maybe tomorrow.'

'Have you asked Eoin about Paris?'

'I hardly see him these days outside of performances and all he ever thinks about is the show; it's like he's living in a parallel universe or something. He doesn't seem to care about anything else. I don't think he's even gone to see Carla.'

'Maybe Nette is putting him off too?'

'Maybe.' Lally watched a bird circling above them. 'I've tried to get him to stand still long enough to ask him about Paris but I know what he'll say – "Have you asked Nette and Carla? What did they say?"'

Gilles said nothing for a moment, then, 'I'm sorry, Lally. I was looking forward to you coming.'

'Me too.'

'Maybe they'll change their minds.'

Lally shook her head. 'Nette says we can't afford it.'

'But every show is full – we're turning people away.'

'You know what's really weird? About what Carla said about me going to Paris and getting away from *Beetle*?'

'What?'

'I'm not sure she meant *Beetle*. She said "get away from her". At the time I thought she meant *Beetle* 'cause she was looking in *Beetle*'s direction, but...'

'But what?' Gilles sat up and so did Lally. He stared at her. 'Who did she mean if not *Beetle*?'

'I think she might have meant—'

A heavy *thunk* on *Beetle*'s roof made Lally turn her head. A jackdaw had landed nearby. Gilles leaned back on his elbows and watched it watching them.

'Do you think it's the same one every time?' he asked.

Lally nodded. She felt suddenly cold. 'Shoo! Shoo, creepy bird.' She waved her arms at it but it didn't budge, just stared back at them.

'You know the stuff about hawthorn trees on the Internet?' Lally said, suddenly unable to stop herself. 'It said that hawthorns were connected with witches and the familiars of hawthorn witches were crows. And guess when that jackdaw started hanging around the barge?'

'When?'

'The day after we took the tree trunk onboard.' Lally tried to keep her voice light, like she was just joking. Which she was. Wasn't she?

'Cool!' Gilles laughed. 'That's a really cool coincidence. Hey, bird!'

The jackdaw turned towards Gilles's voice.

'Are you here for the hawthorn?'

The jackdaw's eyes swivelled away from them. A man

and a woman were coming down the steps from the street. The woman smiled at Lally and Gilles.

'Is this the Theatre Barge?' she asked, even though there was a sign which clearly said that it was.

Lally nodded.

'May we speak with the proprietor?'

Lally knocked on the roof. 'Eoin,' she called. 'Someone to see you.'

There was no response.

'Hold on a sec,' Lally said to the man and woman. 'He is in there.' She stood up and walked along the roof, leaped onto the stern and tripped down the stairs.

'Eoin?' She looked around the chow house. 'Eoin?'

She knocked on his cabin door. 'Eoin? Are you in there?'

She heard a groan and some shuffling. A moment later her dad opened the door and stared out at her sleepily.

'Were you in bed?' she asked, rather unnecessarily.

He nodded and leaned against the door jamb. 'What is it?' His voice was slurred and gruff.

'People to see you.' She nodded towards the path. 'Are you all right, Eoin?'

'What? Oh, yeah, sure.' He pulled his long-sleeved T-shirt over his head but not quickly enough. Those odd little puncture marks were still on his arms. They looked sore.

'Eoin?' Lally asked. 'What's going on?'

'I've was writing all last night so now I'm whacked, that's all.'

'A new play?' Lally asked.

He nodded and yawned.

'But those marks on your arms—'

'What do these people want? Did they say?' Eoin flattened his hair with his hands and brushed past her through the chow house without waiting for an answer.

At the door the woman thanked Lally and turned a beaming smile on Eoin. It was obvious that she and the man expected Lally to go away now. Suddenly curious and annoyed all rolled into one, Lally considered acting dumb and standing her ground but she heard the tinkling call of an ice-cream van. Gilles caught her eye and beckoned to her.

When they came back down to the poolside with their half-eaten cones the man and woman were leaving.

'Thanks again,' the woman said, as she passed them on the steps. 'Be seeing you.'

At the barge Eoin was grinning from ear to ear. There was a sparkle in his eyes that Lally hadn't seen much of recently. He did a little skip and jump as they approached, and rubbed his hands together.

'So,' he said. 'What do you guys think of working with shorter strings?'

TWENTY-TWO

'Shorter strings?' Nette spluttered. She, Des and Claudine had joined Lally and Gilles outside to hear Eoin's news. 'You mean, perform without a bridge? Why would we do that?'

'So that we can do an open-air performance in front of a larger audience,' Eoin replied.

'Where?' asked Des. 'And why and when?'

'There. Browning's Island.' Eoin pointed to the island in the middle of the pool. 'Because we've been invited to do so by the local council as part of their summer arts weekend in two weeks' time.'

Everyone began speaking at once and Eoin raised his hands for quiet.

'First of all, it will pay really well. The council will give us a lump sum for taking part. We could make as much from three performances as we normally make in a month. That's not to be sneezed at.' He looked around for consensus on this. Claudine and Des nodded. Nette frowned impatiently. Lally looked at Gilles, wide-eyed. He mouth-shrugged back at her but she could see he was interested in what Eoin was saying.

And so am I, she thought. It sounds amazing.

But she couldn't believe Eoin was suggesting this.

Eoin, champion of the traditional way, suggesting they cut the strings?

'Let me get this straight. You're suggesting we do a performance out in the open?' Des stroked his chin and pursed his lips.

'Yes.' Eoin nodded. 'We'll perform on the island itself. It will be our stage. Our audience will come on the trip boats that work on the canal, which, as you know, have their own seating. But the council are also going to provide a big screen and a cameraman so that more people can watch from the towpath. They'll look after all the safety stuff and provide the stage, and the lighting and sound systems.'

'It's going to be filmed?'

'Yes.'

'And all of us will be visible, walking about the stage, working the puppets at arm height?'

'Yes.' Eoin's eyes flickered from Des to Nette and back again.

'No bridge?'

'No.'

Des leaned back against the *Beetle*, folded his arms and pulled a face.

'We always said we'd never do that,' Nette said. 'We're a traditional company working the puppets in the traditional way. Never let the hand on the string be seen, that's what you always say.'

'This is a one-off,' Eoin insisted. 'Anyway, it's time we embraced the real world, Nette. There's a fashion for this kind of puppetry now – we should at least try it.'

'So we just switch from a lifetime of working the puppets from a bridge to walking about on stage with them? And what about the scenery and the props?'

'We can afford to take a few days out before the festival to prepare.' Eoin spoke slowly as if Nette was being particularly stupid. 'The whole story takes place on a lake.' He swung his arm in an arc. 'Hey presto, a lake. And we can adapt the props.'

Des looked thoughtful but Nette exploded.

'We can't do it, there isn't time. And what's more, we *shouldn't* do it! Who the hell cares what the latest fashion is? It's not how we work. And we're already one pair of hands short with Carla laid up. No. It's ridiculous. Every time we settle into one thing we switch to another. I don't know what's got into you this summer, Eoin, but it's not happening.'

'I've already bloody well said yes,' Eoin shouted, losing it completely at last.

Lally blanched. He'd been argumentative and bad-humoured all summer but she'd never seen him like this, yo-yoing from excited to furious. Spittle was actually spraying from his mouth.

Nette was so astonished she opened her mouth and closed it again.

'That's not how we make decisions on board *Beetle*, Eoin, you know that.' Des spoke quietly but Lally could see he had brought her dad up short.

'Fine. We'll vote on it then,' Eoin said, making a visible effort to rein in his anger. He pursed his lips, shoved his hands in his pockets and stared at the ground. 'May I just point out first that we do need the money and that this is a way for my – *our* work to reach a much bigger audience, possibly hundreds of people. That has to count for something. Claudine. How do you vote?'

'Oh, well…' Claudine blinked rapidly. 'I have to admit I would love it. Everything about it. It would be interesting to learn to use the puppets that way. And I would really like to get over to Browning's Island; it is very romantic.' She smiled apologetically at Nette.

'Gilles?'

'Yes, *oui*, I'm for it.' Gilles's answer came quick and sure.

'Lally?' Eoin turned to her. His blue eyes were almost feverishly bright. He's really got his heart set on this, Lally thought. But Nette hates the whole idea.

She frowned.

I can't please them both; I'll just have to please myself.

'Yes. I'm for it,' she said, avoiding Nette's eyes.

'Des?'

They all looked at the older man. He shook his head and Eoin's face fell.

'You won't do it?' Eoin said sourly.

'I can't believe I'm saying this.' Des hesitated and

shook his head again. 'But, yes. Yes, I will do it. It's a challenge, something new.'

Eoin beamed at him and they all turned to Nette.

'Well, I'm outvoted, aren't I? I suppose I've no choice.' Her voice shook slightly. 'One way or other, my first responsibility will be looking after Carla, so I'll not be taking on anything extra. Let's be clear on that.'

'That's fine,' Eoin said. He reached a hand out to squeeze her shoulder but Nette pulled away. 'It'll be good for us, Nette,' he said. 'The extra money won't go amiss and it's huge publicity. This is just what we need.'

She gave a curt nod, turned on her heel and went back aboard *Ladybird*. Everyone watched her go. Lally felt uncomfortable, as if she'd let Nette down. But she really did want to do this show; it sounded so very, very cool.

'Well,' Eoin said. 'I think we should celebrate. Is that ice-cream van still about? The ninety-nines are on me.'

The 13th day of June, in the year of our Lord, 1596

I have worked hard these past weeks trying to prove myself to my new employer, Master Spragge. He is an accountant and I assist him with the keeping of his books.

I'm happy here.

I am.

The hours are long but regular. The work is tedious but well within my reach. I would never have made a playwright but may, one day, aspire to set up for myself as an accountant. And Cheapside is a pleasant enough area, not so rough and wild as Southwark. Honey Lane is as safe as any street you'll find in London. Here the night watchmen patrol with their dogs and their lamps, bidding folk put out their fires and lock up their houses.

The rhythm of life in this house calms my jangled nerves. Master Spragge is a devout man, strict and frugal. He never frequents the local tavern and I must follow his example. That is no great penance to me. I spend the evenings with the family, eating good simple food, and listening to Beatrice Spragge, the eldest daughter, reading aloud from the Bishop's Bible. Whenever she glances up and catches me staring at her, she smiles gently and blushes.

No, I do not regret the leaving of Southwark at all. I only wish I could blot out all memory of that tyme. I swear I wish I'd never been in Master Waller's employ, nor never known Bennet and Tom.

That morning in May when I left Southwark the bridge was already busy, filling up with the first shoppers of the day. As I walked the bustling thoroughfare, pressing through the crowd, I recognised some local thieves and rogues amongst them, looking for an easy mark. I spotted a young lad gawping about him at the bridge, staring at all the fine houses and shops perched upon it. He minded me of myself when I first arrived in London many months ago.

It is a wonderous sight, London Bridge. A whole town's worth of the finest buildings, finer than any that lad will ever have seen, and all of them strung in a line on the widest bridge in all the land, high above the water which rushes through the piers on its way to the sea. It scarce seems possible that such a thing could exist, yet there it is, full of people shopping at its fancy shops and stalls.

Fresh come to London, poor Bacon, I thought, looking at the pink-faced lad. No doubt he imagines he'll make his fortune here. These Londoners will chew him up and spit him out, like they've done me. Well, I'll not be that naive misfit any longer.

I passed him at the north bridge-gate, still gazing about himself, slack-mouthed with wonder, as one of the cutpurses closed in on him. Then and there I swore

I'd not look back the way I'd come. I'd leave my theatre misadventures behind me and begin anew.

In Saint Paul's Cathedral all was the usual bustle. The long nave was thronged with people gossiping and doing business and children playing games. In the centre were a group of men and women available for work and I went and stood with them.

That's how I come to be in this house. Master Spragge came to Paul's Walk that day looking for a scrivener and, as luck would have it, I was the only one for hire. He interviewed me right there in the nave. His one doubt on employing me was whether I could possibly be of sound character, having risked my moral fortitude by working amongst theatre folk in Southwark. It was stupid of me to mention Master Waller – I should have pretended that I was just arrived from the country. London is a huge place, not a little gossiping town like Chiswick; Master Spragge would never have known I was lying. But I am not much practised at dissembling; I was out with it before I could stop myself.

'I-I never fitted in,' I added quickly, keeping my head bent respectfully, the better to hide my careful twisting of the truth. 'I w-wasn't happy there. They were strange folk. Master Waller ended my employment on a whim!'

I thank God he believed me. I have left the past behind now. I'm happy here, in my new position amongst the kindly Spragges in Honey Lane.

I do not wonder what's become of Master Waller. I do not worry about the fate of him that tossed me out into the street. His welfare is none of my concern.

187

TWENTY-THREE

R ehearsals for the Browning's Island shows were to take place up on *Beetle*'s roof and the first lot were a bit of a disaster. Everyone, Eoin included, struggled with the shorter strings.

Standing upright with the puppets dangling about your legs wasn't at all normal, Lally decided. And being visible was just plain weird.

An audience of silent teenagers and a couple of mums with pushchairs gathered in the sunshine, and everyone aboard *Beetle* become self-conscious. Lally fumbled and dropped her swan child. It took ten minutes to untangle the strings. Then Gilles overdid a flying movement and two swans clashed, causing more tangles. It was all a bit embarrassing, particularly when Claudine fell overboard.

It was one of those slow-motion things. She had stepped backwards mid-action and her foot had caught the edge of the roof. There was a split-second when it could have gone either way but Claudine used it to toss her puppet to safety. Two big windmill actions with her arms couldn't help her then, and she disappeared to portside with a shriek. The teenagers broke into applause.

'Nice one!' they called, punching each other and folding up, helpless with laughter. 'D'you see that? Encore!'

The two mums giggled and moved away.

'I guess that ends our rehearsals for now,' Eoin grumbled, as Gilles and Des tried to pull Claudine back onto the deck. They were laughing so much she fell in again and nearly took Gilles with her.

Eoin gathered up the puppets. 'I'll bring these down below before they come a cropper too. Tell everyone to be back here at six sharp.'

Lally went below to fetch some towels. When she returned Claudine was onboard, dripping all over the place.

'Thank you, Lally,' she giggled, picking some green gungy stuff out of her hair.

'We will go for a walk when we've cleaned up here, Lally?' Gilles asked, wiping his wet arms on his jeans.

'Actually, I want to go and see Carla. Do you mind?' Lally said. 'Nette's still acting funny about me visiting so I haven't seen her for a week. Nette's not there right now, she's gone shopping and rehearsals have ended early…'

Gilles smiled. 'Go,' he said. 'I can take the rest of the stuff below. Go. *Allez!*' He gave her a little push. His hand was damp and icy.

'Geroff!' Lally laughed.

She stepped off the barge and walked along the towpath to where *Ladybird* was now moored. Nette had tugged *Bird* apart from *Beetle* a week ago, tying her up about thirty metres away. She said the shows were too noisy for Carla, that every little thing was causing headaches. Since then Lally had only seen Carla out walking with Nette twice and those had been glimpses during show intervals. Nette kept saying Carla was fine but Lally wanted to see for herself.

Bird's door was locked, which was unusual. When Carla didn't answer her knock Lally found the spare key under one of the pot plants and let herself in.

'Carla?' she called as she entered.

Carla was sitting in the same seat she'd been in the last time Lally had seen her, with the same blankets piled around her. The collar was gone and her neck looked thin and fragile without it.

'Who's that?' she asked, squinting.

Lally came closer and switched on a lamp. 'It's me, Lally,' she said.

The woman shook her head. 'No,' she murmured. 'You're not Lally. Lally's gone to Paris.'

Lally felt the breath catch in her throat. 'Carla,' she repeated, squatting down in front of her so their faces were level. 'It's me. Lally.'

Carla looked away. 'Lally is in Paris. Safe in Paris,' she said firmly.

Lally blinked. How could Carla not know who she was? Was this Nette's idea of 'fine'? 'What do you mean, safe?' she asked. 'Safe from what?'

'Safe from her.' Carla's head turned towards *Bird*'s

bows. 'Safe from that creature Eoin brought onto the *Beetle.*'

Lally went cold. Does she mean what I think she means? She can't. It's not possible.

'What creature?' she said carefully. Maybe Carla meant one of Eoin's girlfriends? That must be it. Though there hadn't been anyone since Laura.

Carla pressed her lips together tightly and made a zipping motion with her good hand. 'Nette says I mustn't say it out loud so I shan't. But I know.' She nodded her head. 'I know what I know.' She put her hand under her long dark hair and began to scratch the back of her neck.

Lally stood up and, so Carla couldn't see her distress, turned to the photos hanging on the wall. This has to be something temporary, she thought. I should just play along, not upset her. 'D'you mean Laura? Laura's not here any more. Laura.' She pointed to one of the photos.

Carla shook her head, still rubbing her neck.

'Gemma?' Lally pointed to another photo. 'Sandra?' Lally ran a finger over the oldest image, the one of her mother. 'Elaine?'

'Elaine,' Carla said, without looking at the photograph. 'She was the one.'

'The one Eoin brought on board?'

Carla nodded. 'Found her sleeping rough in ... I can't remember the name of the village ... why can't I remember?' She screwed up her face and hit her forehead with the heel of her hand. 'She was Lally's mum, you know.'

'Yes, I know.'

She knew she shouldn't be asking these questions – Carla was clearly out of it – and yet, she couldn't help herself. 'What was she like? My mu— Elaine.'

'Flibbertigibbet,' Carla said, waving her hand dismissively. 'Young, very young. Eighteen, maybe. Eoin was sorry for her; we all were. Always smoking, even when she was pregnant. And not just cigarettes either. Treated the baby like a doll, a pretty doll. Dressed her up, gave her that silly name. We did all the mothering, me and Nette and Eoin.'

'Well, Eoin is her dad.' Oh, great, Lally thought, now I'm talking about myself in the third person.

Carla raised her eyebrows and tapped her nose with her forefinger. 'Maybe,' she whispered. 'Maybe not.'

Lally's knees buckled and she sat down abruptly on the bench.

Stop asking questions now, she told herself. She doesn't know what she's saying. She doesn't even know I'm me.

But it was too late to stop. She needed to know.

'What do you mean?' she heard herself ask.

Carla began to rub her neck again. 'She said the baby was Eoin's but that would mean she gave birth a month before she was due. And Lally was a small newborn, but not that small.' She shrugged. 'No one said anything. We all fell in love with Lal as soon as we saw her. We wanted her to belong to us. So we never said anything.' She rubbed her neck harder. 'We changed the nappies, made the feeds, cuddled her when she cried. We heard her first words, saw her first steps. And one day Elaine just took off...' She detached her hand from her neck and swept it outwards. 'We said nothing. And they never came to take her.'

'Who? Who never came?' The words came out all choked. Oh God, this couldn't be true, could it? Carla was hallucinating or something.

'Them.' Carla was picking at it now, that spot under her hair. She seemed to lose her train of thought. She stared at Lally. 'Who are you?' she asked, suddenly alarmed. 'Have you come to take her away?'

'Why would I take her away?'

'Because there's no papers, nothing that says she's Eoin's. She was born on the *Beetle* in the middle of nowhere. There's no birth certificate. Nothing.'

Eoin might not be my dad, Lally thought frantically. My mother was a pot-smoking flibbertigibbet. I have no birth certificate.

She gripped the sides of the bench.

Is that why Nette was so adamant I couldn't go to Paris? If I have no birth certificate I won't be able to get a passport.

'Water gypsies,' Carla murmured. 'We're water gypsies. We belong nowhere in particular, so no one keeps track of us. All these years and no one's ever come checking on Lally. They don't even know she exists.'

She took her hand away from her neck and stared at her fingers. 'Blood,' she said.

'What?' Lally leaned across and grabbed Carla's hand. There *was* blood on her fingers, quite a lot of it. Carla pulled her hand free and began to reach back under her hair.

'Don't,' Lally said, jumping to her feet. 'Let me see.'

Carla dropped her hand into her lap and bent her head forward. Lally gently lifted the dark hair to one side. She looked closer, parting the hair, wiping the blood away with a tissue she took from her pocket. It was trickling from just inside the hairline.

What was that? Something black just under the skin. She pinched it with her finger and thumb. Carla winced and shoved her away.

'Stop,' she whimpered.

'You have a splinter or something stuck in your neck, Carla,' Lally said. 'It's obviously hurting you. It needs to come out, OK?'

Carla drew her knees towards her and curled good arm around bad. There was a very slight head movement which could have meant yes.

'Right,' Lally said in what she hoped was a soothing voice. 'I'll find some tweezers.'

TWENTY-FOUR

'Lally. What are you doing here?' Nette appeared in the doorway just as Lally found a pair of tweezers in a jar of make-up brushes. 'How did you get in?'

'The spare key.' Lally looked Nette straight in the eyes. 'Carla isn't well. You've been telling us all she just needs rest and that she's fine. She's not.'

Nette let the bags of shopping slide to the floor around her. 'What's she been saying?'

Blurt it out, Lally thought. Ask if it's true. You have a right to know.

'Carla doesn't know who I am,' Lally began. 'She said—'

'Oh, Lal.' Nette buried her head in her hands and began to cry. 'I'm so scared. I brought her back to the hospital but they insisted there was no sign of a head injury. They think she's having a breakdown. They wanted to put her into a psychiatric ward. I thought if I could bring her home and keep her quiet and let her recover...' She caught her breath. 'What exactly has she been saying? Has she been going on about the puppet again?'

'Which puppet?' Lally held her breath. She knew exactly which puppet.

'The puppet Eoin made from the hawthorn wood. She blames everything on it. She says it caused the accident. How crazy is that? She keeps saying you need to be protected from her.'

'She thinks I'm in Paris.'

'I know.' Nette swiped her hand across her cheek and sniffed. 'I'm sorry, Lal. I didn't want you to see her like this.'

Tell her what Carla said, Lally thought. Questions were flying around her head. She just wanted to blurt them out and make Nette give her some answers.

But Nette's face. Nette's face was so anxious. Lally couldn't do it. Not right now.

She bit her lip and tried to hide the turmoil on her face. Surely Nette could see how upset she was? But Nette was preoccupied with Carla.

Lally held up the tweezers. 'There's something in her neck, a splinter. It's really irritating her. I'm going to get it out.' She stepped over the shopping bags and went back into the living space.

Nette held Carla's hand as Lally located the thing beneath her skin again. 'This is going to hurt, Carla,' Lally said. 'But I'll try and be really quick.'

The splinter resisted her first and second try – it almost seemed to be digging itself in deeper – but it came out on the third. Lally held it up to the light. It was long and dark, slender as a sewing needle.

'Oh, wow,' Nette exclaimed, examining the wound. 'It's infected, there's pus. Fetch me the first aid box, Lal.'

196

Lally wrapped the splinter in a piece of tissue and slipped it into her jeans pocket. The first aid box was under the sink. She handed it to Nette.

'I've got to go,' she said.

And she did. If she stayed here one moment longer she wouldn't be able to hold it in, what Carla had said about Eoin not being her dad. She'd have to ask, demand the truth. It wouldn't be fair; Nette had enough pain and worry as it was, so the best thing was to go. Bite her tongue and go.

'Sure, love,' Nette said, without looking up from Carla's bleeding neck. 'I'm so glad you came, pet. I've checked her neck so often the last few days to see what on earth was agitating her. I just couldn't see anything. It took young eyes, eh?'

'Yeah.' Lally waved at Carla. 'Guess so.'

'Lally,' the older woman said, as if she was seeing her for the first time. 'Lally, is that you?'

'Yes, it's me, Carla,' Lally said, her voice wobbling. 'I'm just leaving.'

Carla smiled, then reached out and patted Lally's hand. 'I know,' she said. 'You grow up and you go your own way. That's how it should be.'

'She's only going back to the *Beetle*, Carla,' Nette said in a soothing voice. But Carla didn't seem upset. Her eyes were quite focused as she looked at Lally.

'You grow up and go your own way,' she repeated. 'That's how it should be.'

TWENTY-FIVE

U p on the towpath Lally looked at her watch. Five
thirty. There was no one about but rehearsals
were due to start again in half an hour so Eoin would
appear any minute.

I can't see him now, she thought. I just can't.

She needed to be alone. She put her hand to her
back pocket and pulled out a folded-up bank note. Des
had had a rare win on the horses the other day and
he'd given her a twenty.

'I notice you're developing a bit of a café habit, you
and young Gilles,' he'd said with a smile. 'You'll be
needing some pocket money to keep up with him, eh?'

She pushed the money back into her pocket.

I've got to get out of here, she told herself, just go.
Now.

Then she was running under the bridge, up the steps,
across the street, up Warwick Avenue. She slowed to
a walk about halfway along but didn't stop. The tube
station was ahead.

At the station she took the same line as she had that
day with Gilles and Claudine. It was rush hour so she
had to stand. She felt as if everyone was looking at her,
as if everyone knew that she was running away.

Is that what I'm doing? she thought. Am I running away? Yes. At least for a few hours. It'll mess up rehearsals, but I need to think. I need to work this out.

She tried to stop catching other passengers' eyes and stared over their heads at the ads that ran above the windows. She settled on the underground map and ticked the tube station names off as they passed through each one. She'd get off at Waterloo and walk along the river, like before.

Eoin might not be my dad.

Is that why she called him Eoin? She'd always figured it was because everyone around her did – Des, Nette and Carla, Eoin's girlfriends, the visiting trainees – so she did too. Had she ever called him Dad? Had he even taught her to?

Eoin might not be my dad.

She repeated the words in her head over and over.

It couldn't be true, could it?

The only way to find out would be to ask.

It would upset everyone if it was true. Maybe she shouldn't say anything. But she needed to know. She had a right to know.

Who could she ask? Nette was too upset about Carla right now. Des? Would he know? Would he say so if he did? Des always said mind your own business and let everyone else mind theirs.

Eoin. It would have to be Eoin.

But Eoin was so distant these days. How would she even get his attention?

Well he'd just have to get his head out of his play and that horrible puppet for long enough to hear what she had to say. If she had to scream it at him, she would. Her anger was so sudden and strong she was sure the whole carriage could feel it. She squeezed her eyes shut.

Don't cry. Not here. Don't cry at Waterloo.

A snort of laughter tangled itself with a half-sob and came out as a cough. The doors opened and there was a surge of bodies towards the platform.

'Mind the gap,' said the intercom as Lally let herself be swept towards the escalator.

On street level the crowds were walking purposefully and impatiently. Lally took a deep breath and joined the flow towards the riverside. People were a bit more relaxed along the walk, tourists strolling or people sitting having after-work drinks. She went to the wall and leaned over, looking at the Thames, in the same place as she and Claudine and Gilles had eaten chips that day.

The day Carla had her accident.

What had Nette said earlier? *'Has she been going on about the puppet again? She blames everything on it. She says it caused the accident. How crazy is that?'*

Was it crazy? All the weirdness this summer had started with that piece of wood. In seven weeks Eoin had changed from her easy-going, good-humoured dad to a surly monosyllabic introvert who kept to his cabin when he wasn't onstage (and he might not be her dad at all, let's not forget that bit). Nette, who was normally so forthright and strong, was telling half-truths and crying. Carla was amnesiac and delusional.

And the accident. Carla had been arguing with Eoin about the witch puppet and the play when it happened, and from where Lally had been sitting it had seemed as though the witch-of-the-air had attacked the swan, causing Carla to fall.

Lally pulled the splinter out of her front pocket. It was still intact. She touched the point with her fingertip.

Ow!

She almost opened her fingers and let the splinter drop to the ground.

What if someone steps on it? she thought. Nearly everyone's wearing sandals. She wrapped the splinter in the tissue again and put it back in her pocket.

She could toss it in a bin in a minute.

But she knew she wouldn't. Not yet. Not till she was sure it hadn't come from where she thought it had. At least she could find out the answer to that question easily enough. And right now her head ached from too many unanswered questions.

On her left a young guy in a suit lit up a cigarette.

'Can I have one?' Did she just say that out loud?

The man raised an eyebrow but he held out the packet.

'Thanks,' she said.

'D'you need a light?'

She shook her head. 'Thanks,' she said again. She held the cigarette loosely inside her fist and walked away. There was a shop near here, a newsagent she remembered from before. She went in and pointed to a lighter decorated with a drawing of old London Bridge, the medieval one that had had all the buildings on it. The bridge from the nursery rhyme; the one that had fallen down.

'It's for my mum,' she said.

The shop assistant shrugged.

'And I'll take these.' Lally picked up two cans of Spinner, the drink that was supposed to have so much caffeine in, it gave you a sort of high.

She still had enough for a bag of chips. She'd get them later in the chippy Claudine had taken them to. That'd leave just enough for her train back. She should have bought a return ticket.

Because she'd go back to Little Venice eventually, though not for a few hours. Not till it was dark. Not till it felt like she'd been gone long enough to at least think of this as the day she ran away.

And she'd smoke this stupid cigarette.

What had Carla said about her mother?

That she was always smoking.

Eoin must have hated that; he hated smoking. He'd made Lally promise never to do it.

She walked a little further along the riverbank. This bit was all cafés and restaurants but there was an area further up where the walk opened out into a public space. She found a corner, uncurled her fist from around the cigarette and flicked the lighter open. Her hands shook a little as she put the cigarette between

202

her lips and brought the flame to meet it. She inhaled. The flame didn't catch the first time. It did the second.

TWENTY-SIX

In the end she caught the nine o'clock train because she'd started to get cold. As she approached the *Beetle* she could see the barge was in darkness. Where was everyone?

Out looking for me. She felt a twinge at the thought. They'll all be worried sick. Well, maybe it's time they stopped treating me like a kid and let me have my own mobile phone.

She dug her hands into her pockets to keep them warm as she approached the boat. The splinter jabbed her fingers.

Ah, I forgot; let's go see if I'm right about you.

She took the splinter out and held it up in the yellow light of the street lamp. It wasn't the colour of any of the wooden bits onstage. The stage floor was painted black and none of the puppets were this shade of wood.

Except the witch puppet. The puppet Eoin had made from the hawthorn wood was reddish-brown.

She'd be in her usual place, hanging in Eoin's cabin.

Lally hesitated. She'd done all sorts of un-Lally things today; she might as well do one more. She opened *Beetle*'s door, switched on the lights and went down the stairs. She turned right in the chow house, and tried the handle to Eoin's cabin.

Locked. Well, as on *Bird*, she knew exactly where to find the spare keys. She went to the galley and reached into a cupboard. The spares were where they always were, inside a chipped mug at the back of the shelf.

But when she stood outside the cabin door the lock resisted the key. Each time Lally tried to slip it into the keyhole, she missed and it slid away across the door.

Too much Spinner, she thought.

Her hands were trembling. She kneeled and carefully inserted the key, sticking her tongue between her teeth as if she was threading a needle.

The key wouldn't turn.

She tried forcing it, she tried guiding it. She tried pulling the door towards herself, she tried pushing it away. Determined, she went and fetched pliers from Des's toolbox. She pinched the head of the key between the pliers and forced the thing to turn.

OK. I'm in. She pushed down on the handle. But the door seemed to resist her too.

Like that night a month ago, she thought. The night Eoin was carving and she'd tried to knock on his door. The night she'd thought she'd only dreamed.

She put all her weight against the door and suddenly it gave. She fell in after it and landed on the floor. There was paper everywhere, in untidy piles scattered around the lino and the desk. In the light from the corridor she could make out Eoin's untidy scrawl.

No wonder he's so grumpy. He can't be getting much

sleep if he's doing this every night.

She got to her feet intending to flick the light switch but as she straightened up something caught a lock of her hair. She jerked away and it held fast, catching more hair as she struggled. She stood still but the tugging didn't stop. She jerked away, turning as she went.

The witch puppet's eyes gazed coldly at her from the shadows.

'You!' Lally said aloud.

The witch was suspended from the roof, her wings unfurled, her white mask hanging by her side. Her face was almost level with Lally's.

'I'm not afraid of you,' Lally said. 'Carla may be, but I'm not.' She reached behind her and switched the light on.

'Does this belong to you?' She held up the splinter. 'Let's see, shall we?'

She reached out to grab the puppet's little hands.

'Ow!' Something like pain whizzed through her fingertips. Had there been green sparks?

'Too much caffeine,' she said. 'I've had too much caffeine.'

She took the hands in hers again and ignored the buzzing working its way from her fingertips along her arms.

Caffeine. Caffeine, she repeated to herself. It's just too much caffeine. I AM NOT AFRAID OF YOU.

There it was. A long thin chip out of one of the fingers. She held the splinter up to it and the fit was perfect. Except ... was it actually a splinter? Surely, now she looked closer, it looked more like a long dark thorn?

This time there was no mistaking the green flash. It raced from the puppet's finger to the splinter and circled Lally's arm in a quick bright flame that was there and gone.

'Whah!'

Lally instinctively grabbed at her arm, dropping the sliver of wood. Something loud popped near her ear and the light bulb exploded above her head, pitching the room back into darkness. She ducked and threw her arms up over her face. The thin glass shattered into thousands of tiny pieces and fell on her arms and hair like malevolent confetti. Lally squeezed her eyes shut and frantically shook herself. Behind her eyelids the green flash reconstructed and replayed itself in red.

Flash, flicker, flash.

She snapped her eyes open and pulled her hair back from her eyes. She stared at the puppet, which was now half-hidden in shadow again.

'What are you?' Lally whispered. 'What are you doing to us?'

She stepped backwards out the door. Two hands closed on her arms.

'Where the hell have you been?' Eoin's voice.

He spun her around to face him. He looked furious, distressed and relieved, all at the same time. Over his shoulder Lally saw Des, Claudine and Gilles staring at her.

'She's back safe. We'll go to bed, so,' Des said and they all turned away and melted off towards their rooms.

'Why did you run off like that, Lally?' Eoin gave her a small shake. She glanced back into his room where the puppet was hanging in the shadows.

'What is she?' Lally asked.

'What?'

'That thing you brought on board.' Lally turned to watch his face. 'You've changed since *she* came.'

'Don't be ridiculous.' He frowned, reached around her and pulled his door closed.

'She hurt Carla,' Lally said. 'You know she did.'

Eoin blinked and shielded his eyes as if the lights in the chow house were bothering him. But she'd seen the flicker of recognition. She'd seen it. He knew what she meant. He absolutely knew.

He shook his head. 'It's late. We've been running around the streets looking for you all night. I'm tired.' He looked at some point on the wall behind her. 'Go to bed, Lally.'

TWENTY-SEVEN

'You OK?' Gilles said softly from his hammock as Lally tiptoed through the dark of the theatre. He flicked on his torch. 'What happened? Why did you take off like that?'

My dad may not be my dad. I don't officially exist. But she couldn't bring herself to say it out loud. Not yet.

'Carla didn't know who I was,' she said. She climbed up to the bench which was level with Gilles's hammock and sat down.

Gilles nodded. 'That's what Nette said. She thought that might have been what upset you. Where'd you go?'

'Southbank. Where we went with your mum.'

Gilles nodded again. 'What did you do?'

'I walked and drank a load of Spinner. And smoked a cigarette.'

He pulled a downward mouth shrug. 'Did you like it?'

She shook her head. 'Nope.'

She looked down at her hand.

'There's something else,' she said. 'Just now, in Eoin's cabin. The witch puppet. I touched her and got some sort of shock. Then the light bulb burst.'

'Static?' he suggested.

'Carla thinks that puppet caused her accident.' She paused. She knew it would sound nuts but she was going to say it anyway. 'I-I think so too.'

Gilles's eyebrows shot up. 'Why?' he said.

'I took a splinter from Carla's neck today. It's from the puppet. It fits her finger.'

Gilles shone the torch into her eyes. 'Just how much Spinner did you have?' he said.

She pushed the torch away. 'I'm serious, Gilles. Ever since that wood came on board *Beetle*, Eoin's been acting funny. You must have noticed. And now everyone is. Well, not Des. Des is just, well, Des.'

'People act funny all the time.'

'No, no. They're usually pretty normal. It's that puppet, I know it is.' She could hear her voice sounding frantic. And she was speaking more quickly than usual. 'All that stuff we looked up about hawthorn trees. It said it's unlucky. It said it's – well, it said—' She faltered. Was she really going to say the word 'faery' out loud? 'I saw a face in the water, Gilles,' she whispered. 'The day we got stuck on the hawthorn tree trunk. I saw a face, her face, the puppet's face.'

'OK.' Gilles frowned but held her gaze.

'And Eoin has strange marks on his arms, Gilles. He said they came from carving the puppet. They're exactly like the wound on Carla's neck.'

'OK.'

'You don't believe me.' Lally bit her lip. 'You think I'm crazy.'

'No. But...' Gilles hesitated. His frown deepened and when he continued speaking his voice was measured and slow. 'Look, puppets are strange things. We give them life and sometimes it feels as if they don't give it back when we hang them up. Look at them.' He pointed to the marionettes decorating the theatre walls. Hippity, Hoppity and Zee, Dog and Cinders. 'Don't they look as if they're waiting? Waiting for the strings to be touched? The more I work with them, the more it feels like I'm not thinking about it any more, as if the strings are moving themselves. Sometimes I look down at the puppet and wonder, "Did I make you do that? Or did you do it yourself?" You know what I mean, *oui*?'

Lally nodded. 'I think that all the time. It's like life is flowing up and down the strings, flowing both ways.' She put her elbows on her knees and lowered her forehead down onto her hands. There was a pain shooting behind her eyes, growing stronger by the minute.

Had she imagined it? What she saw in Eoin's cabin? In Eoin's eyes?

'Is that glass in your hair?' Gilles asked suddenly.

'The light bulb burst,' she said again.

'Hold still; I'll get it out.' He slid off the hammock onto the seat beside her and began to pick carefully over her mass of curls.

She couldn't hold the tears back any longer. They fell down her face into her hands and trickled through her fingers. She reached for her tissue but it was on the floor of Eoin's cabin, with the splinter. He'd probably stand on the splinter and end up with it in his foot. Serve him right.

She sniffed. She didn't mean that. Of course she didn't. But she needed him. She needed to ask him about what Carla had said. She needed him to tell her it wasn't true. For the first time in her life, Eoin wasn't there for her.

'Hey,' Gilles said softly. 'Don't cry.' He pulled a tissue from somewhere and put his arm around her shoulders.

'I didn't imagine it, Gilles,' she whispered. 'What just happened in Eoin's cabin and other stuff that's happened this summer. I've been telling myself I was dreaming or imagining things or being silly but I'm not. There's something really wrong and it's all to do with that puppet. I understand if you don't believe me but I need to say it out loud. OK?'

'OK.' Gilles's eyes were big and serious. 'This is your home, these people are your family. If you say there is something really wrong, then there is.' He nodded. 'I believe this half of what you say,' he said with an apologetic smile.

Lally wiped her eyes with the heel of her hand.

He half-believed her. That was good enough for now.

The 17th day of June, in the year of our Lord, 1596

*T*he flag is flying from the roof of the Rose. The bill posted by the door announces that this afternoon the theatre hosts *Waller's Men* in the second performance of The Death of Faire Frideswide – *a play of five acts. The trumpet has not sounded yet; I am in time for the performance.*

It's my first free day since taking up my apprenticeship with Master Spragge. Sundays are not truly mine as I am obliged to accompany the family to church and sit quietly about the house when not at prayer. It was my intention today to go and look upon the splendour of Westminster Abbey; instead my feet have obstinately taken me the other way, down Gracechurch Street and across the bridge, straight to the entrance of Henslowe's theatre.

I'm only here out of an idle interest to know how Master Waller's newest writing goes. The queue dwindles; I approach and drop my penny in the box.

In the pit I jostle for a space near the middle. Being small of stature I do not want to stand too far back but I do not want to risk catching the eye of any of the players on stage by going too far forward. The middle ground's the place for me. The floor of the pit is sloped so my view is good enough. The hazel shells and straw that cover the ground are spongy 'neath my feet, sodden with yesterday's rain. I cast my eyes skyward. Some clouds are scudding over the theatre, but they do not threaten an imminent downpour. The damp is rising through my shoes but my head should stay dry.

I look about. The pit's capacity is seven hundred and must be near reached, for we groundlings stand simmering together like so many beans in a pot. Up in the galleries which circle the pit and the stage, those who can afford seats under the roof are chattering and drinking ale, scoffing pies and sweetmeats, and renting cushions at a penny a piece. The trumpet sounds and everyone around me presses forward. I step on the woman in front's heels. She turns and glares at me.

'A pox on thee, clumsy baggage!' she snaps, scowling through blackened teeth and painted lips.

I stammer an apology. She opens her mouth to berate me some more but Nashe walks on stage and everyone gives a cheer. The play is begun.

Nashe, as narrator, gives us a short description of what we are about to see. 'Twill be a tragedy of betrayed virtue and false love, as the title suggests. Tom appears then, as Faire Frideswide, bedecked in a golden periwig and an embroidered gown of orange tawny silk. An actor I do not know accompanies him, playing Frideswide's mother. Bennet plays the false suitor, Hobbes is his henchman.

214

Nashe, as well as the narrator's role, plays a rival lord and also a messenger. Three other actors play a host of other parts between them.

At first I am distracted by having to stretch to see the action over the heads of the crowd, and someone keeps digging their elbow in my back. But soon I am carried away by the drama. I am fooled by Bennet's declarations of love, I boo and hiss at Hobbes and shriek with fright when Frideswide is carried off.

The crowd around me seem most satisfied with their entertainment, though there is a strangeness in the language, an uneasy darkness about the story that has people twitching and nudging each other and fiddling with their beards and cuffs. I myself am nibbling anxiously at my nails. Then, as the death scene is enacted, a strange fog rises and rolls across the stage. The crowd are impressed. It is a trick I have not seen before. How has Bennet managed it?

A sound distracts me. The whaff whaff of many bird wings passing overhead. A fractured shadow sweeps across the crowd; everyone looks up.

A murder of crows!

Silently they descend upon the roof and settle on the thatch. How very strange – their presence and their silence, crows being normally most noisesome birds! The actors pause; I note a surreptitious exchange of glances between Bennet and Hobbes. They wait for the crowd to settle again and the play continues. At the last applause the birds burst into the air cawing and cackling, and disperse. There must be four score and twenty of them.

Afterwards I wait in the yard of the George, knowing that the actors will come here when they have taken off their costumes and make-up. I order ale and pie and try to quiet my nerves.

You see, the thought has been creeping in on me this past week, the thought that perhaps it was all some strange fancy on my part after all – the sprite in Master Waller's chamber. My mother has often said I have an over-wrought disposition. I can't have seen what I thought I saw that night; it is impossible. I have to have imagined it. But still I must know – despite all my daily resolutions to the contrary – I must know something of Master Waller's well-being.

I will put up with Bennet's ridicule and Tom's pity just long enough to do that, then I will go back to Honey Lane and a life more suited to my temperament.

'Well, well,' a familiar voice drawls. 'Look who has come a-visiting from the City.'

Bennet regards me with his hands upon his hips and a glint in his eye.

'Told you it was him I saw,' Tom says. 'It was you, Flea? You came to see the play?'

I nod.

'How goes it with Master Spragge?' Bennet asks, with a sly smile as he sits down on the bench beside me. Tom and Hobbes and Nashe arrange themselves opposite.

'How do you know…?' I frown, confused.

'Your new master came a-calling after he took you on,

216

insisting he must speak to Master Waller. He wanted to know the reason for your dismissal. Annie called me to the door to deal with him. I told him Master Waller has a wild temper and a tendency to take easy offence. I said that you had always done your job well but Master Waller seemed to have taken against you for no reason we could comprehend. I bade him keep his voice down for if Master Waller woke and heard your name mentioned he would like as not come down and break our heads. I hinted that the playwright was not moderate in his cups, that he hadn't seen the inside of a church in several years. This horrified good Master Spragge and sent him off well-pleased that he was not mistaken in you and had rescued you from a bad master besides. In short, I lied on your behalf.' Bennet inclines his head and twirls his wrist. 'You may say thank you, Bennet,' he declares in that mocking tone of his.

'Thank you, Bennet,' I echo, humbly. 'The play goes well?'

'It does. You liked it?'

'I cannot say exactly that I liked it.' I pause to collect the right words to describe my reaction to the tragedy of Frideswide. 'I was much moved. I was shocked by the violence. I was ... disturbed by the atmosphere and the language.'

Bennet ponders this. 'Yes, that sounds about right! It is a strange play by a strange man.' He leans in close and the others follow suit. 'What happened that night in the work chamber, Flea?' he whispers.

I drop my eyes down to my half-eaten pie. 'Nothing,' I

say. 'Nothing happened. I fell asleep and had a nightmare; no doubt it was the cheese I ate at supper.'

Bennet frowns. 'Now, Flea,' he says. 'I've lied for you; do not lie to me. Something happened; out with it.'

He seems sincere but then he is an actor. I will not fall into his trap; I will not be his fool again.

I clear my throat. 'How is Master Waller?' I ask. 'He is well?'

Hobbes and Nashe exchange looks, Tom snorts and Bennet narrows his eyes to impatient slits.

'Master Waller writes well, earns well, is well spoken of,' says Bennet. 'Some say he is almost the equal of Master Shakespeare.'

'And his health?' I ask.

'Ah, his health!' Bennet strokes his moustache. 'Tom! What say you of Master Waller's health?'

Tom snorts again. 'I say,' says he, pausing his cup on its journey to his lip. 'I say Master Waller's health is vigorous, for he surely runs to madness.'

'There you have it, dear Flea!' Bennet puts his arm around my shoulder. 'My lies to Master Spragge were not so short of truth as to be of the blackest kind. I made out that we work for a drunkard and a degenerate. In fact, we work for a lunatic, as crazed as any poor soul locked in Bedlam.'

'You saw the crows?' Tom asks.

I nod.

'Evil birds,' Nashe says, shuddering. 'We've had the pleasure of their attendance at two different plays now.

They always arrive for the last act. The rest of the day and night, they reside on our roof. They came soon after you left.'

'And now Master Waller writes only with crow quills.' Tom scowls. 'I have to gather them up every morning from about the gutters.'

'We are forbidden to eat songbirds! Have you ever heard such a thing?' Hobbes demands, his bushy eyebrows jumping about in outrage. 'What right has he to say what we may eat? No larks, no blackbirds, no thrushes!' He snatches up my abandoned pie and takes a huge bite which sends bits of food tumbling into the ruff about his neck. 'And Annie has left. When the crows came she said that the house had grown cursed and she'd not stay in it another night, so we are obliged to eat every meal here in the George, or starve.'

I almost smile at the thought of Hobbes going hungry.

'And the fog,' says Tom. 'That comes creeping every day too. The Theatre and the Swan beg us for our secret but it is none of our doing.'

''Tis odd – the crows, the fog – but what have they to do with Master Waller?' I venture, determined to draw out more of their suspicions before I admit to them what I saw that night, before I allow myself to own it to myself again.

'Master Waller keeps entirely to the work chamber now, sleeps there, eats there,' Bennet says, his eyes as serious as I've ever seen them. 'He never changes clothes, doesn't trim his beard. He looks like a wild man of the woods, and stinks too! He barely speaks to us and, when he does, he rasps as one whose voice is over-used. His eyes – always so pale – have grown dark and burn like he's been struck with plague. He rubs at his arms as if they are covered in plague buboes.'

'You think this play was strange?' asks Nashe. 'You should read what he's writing now. It is so dark and irreligious I fear the Master of the Revels will not pass it fit for performance.'

'He writes like a man possessed.' Bennet purses his lips. 'Four plays in such a short time, each one more brilliant than the last. From where has this sudden burst of talent come?'

'From him spending more time in his cups and less at his prayers?' I ask, feigning innocence. 'He is writing and writing well; why worry from whence it comes?'

Bennet guffaws and cuffs me playfully across an ear. Not so playfully that it does not hurt a little. 'Mock me with my own words! I deserve it.' He bows graciously. 'I'll allow that I cared not for Master Waller's health when I thought too much ale was all that ailed him. But that is not what he sickens of, is it, Flea?' The smile leaves his lips and he drops his voice. 'We've all heard him through the door, heard him whispering. And we've all seen the strange green will o' the wisp light flickering around his work-chamber door and window; we've all heard the singing, all felt its weird power.' He gives an involuntary shiver and looks straight at me. 'Some strange poison is seeping out of that chamber. It sucks the light from the walls and makes the air fetid and dank, even on the hottest summer day. Waller is infected; I think he is dying. Now, for the love of God, will you tell us what you saw that night?'

'You saw her fingers pierce his skin?' Hobbes shudders and crosses himself, though he is not of the old religion.

'She was a sprite one moment and a creature of solid flesh another,' I say. 'Her fingers drew his blood and her light grew stronger while she drank. He groaned like a man in pain, yet as her light strengthened it seemed to make him write all the faster.'

'As if this evil creature feeds his imagination as she feeds off him,' Bennet suggests and leans back, tapping his forefinger against his mouth.

'That's what I think,' I say.

'That's hideous,' Tom says.

'Hideous,' repeats Nashe, pushing his tankard away as if his thirst has deserted him.

'You – you believe me?' I stammer. 'You believe I saw what I saw?'

They nod their heads. Nashe pats me on the back. I'm close to tears with the relief of it. I am not grown mad; I am not a fool.

We all fall silent.

'What's to be done?' asks Hobbes, at last.

'We must part Master Waller from his muse,' Bennet says. 'We brought the thing within the house; we must get rid of it before it's too late to save the man.'

'He keeps his chamber locked and has both the keys. If we break in and steal the cursed thing he'll have us arrested.

We'll get our ears cropped for our pains, or have our noses slit.' Tom protests, patting his ears and nose as if to reassure them.

'What if we draw him out of that chamber?' I say slowly. 'What if we get him to bring the wretched thing out himself?'

'Zounds! How will we do that?' Hobbes booms.

Bennet raises a finger to his lips and bids him quiet down. 'You have an idea, Flea?' he whispers to me. 'Pray thee, out with it!'

TWENTY-EIGHT

'Throw the bow line,' Des shouted, switching on the engines. 'Let's get moving.'

On the towpath Gilles undid the line and tossed it to Claudine. He gave the bow a shove and jumped on board as the *Beetle* started to shift away.

'OK, Lal,' Des said.

Lally jumped on with the stern line in her arms and the barge began the short trip across the pool. It was Thursday afternoon. Time to bring the *Beetle* over to Browning's Island and get everything set up for the festival shows. Des leaned on the tiller and steered the *Beetle* in a wide arc, around the island to a spot where she would be hidden by the willows but within easy reach of the stage.

A team of people had been working on the island since early that morning constructing the small raised wooden platform. Lally could see they were putting up the stage lighting now. Someone else was up a ladder weaving strings of fairy lights amongst the willows.

'It's going to be beautiful,' Claudine said. 'I wish I wasn't so nervous.' She laughed.

'Me too,' Lally said automatically.

But she wasn't nervous about the show. Her head

was too full of other stuff to worry about performing. Rehearsals today had gone fine anyway. The gathering of teenagers and mums with toddlers had proved useful in helping them all get over their anxiety about being visible. *The Children of Lir* seemed to thrive on tension. Claudine was right; it was going to be beautiful. Even Nette thought so.

Two men on the island stepped forward to catch the lines and tie *Beetle* up in the position she would keep for the weekend. Tomorrow night would be the first of the three shows. This evening was the last run-through, a chance to sort the stage lights and see how the show would look here in the trees.

'Can people start bringing things up, please?' Eoin appeared from below, his arms full of stage bits. 'We haven't got all night.'

Des regarded Eoin, one hand still resting on the *Beetle*'s tiller. 'We've plenty of time,' he said. 'Take it easy. You look like hell, by the way.'

Eoin didn't respond, just dumped his load and went below for more. Des raised his eyebrows and looked at Lally.

'He looks like hell,' he said again.

Lally bit her lip and nodded.

'You're not looking so great yourself, love,' Des said. 'What's up?'

'Nervous about the play, that's all,' Lally said over her shoulder as she passed him on her way down the stairs.

Soon, she thought. When this is over, I'm asking them all to talk to me. All of them, together. Carla's better now, almost back to herself since I took that thing out of her neck.

She had the questions rehearsed in her head. 'Is Eoin my father?' and 'Do I officially exist?' sounded very bald but in the end she had decided being direct would be the best approach. She mustn't give them any chance to sidetrack her.

Soon, she'd get her answers; very soon. But not yet. There was something she had to do first. She knew that now. She'd thought it through carefully and it was the only way.

'Take these.' Eoin held out two of the swan puppets without actually looking her in the eye. As she took the puppets off him he absentmindedly shoved up one of his sleeves and began to scratch.

The marks were still there, the little puncture marks she'd seen weeks ago. Gilles arrived down the stairs behind her and she heard his intake of breath. He'd seen the marks too.

Des was right. Eoin did look awful. His face was grey and his eyes were bloodshot, like he hadn't slept in days. He saw them staring at his arm now and pulled down his sleeve. 'What are you waiting for?' he snapped. 'Like I said, we haven't got all bloody night.'

It took two hours to get the whole thing set up and test the lights and sound. To either side of the stage there were screened areas which would hide the puppeteers when they were not performing in a scene. They also hid the props and a stand which Des had made with hooks for the puppets to hang from when not in use. It was a bit like a coat rack on wheels.

This was to be a full rehearsal so everyone went below to change. They would all be dressed in black and would work on stage in their bare feet. Lally pulled on her leggings and top, and tied her hair back with a bandanna. On *Beetle*'s deck they all gathered with their puppets. Eoin came up with the hawthorn puppet in his arms.

You, thought Lally with a shiver. You've cast some sort of spell on him. You're making him sick.

'Kak!' said a voice above her head. The jackdaw was perched in the willow. Its blue eyes swivelled from her to the puppet and back again. 'Kak,' it said sternly. Lally glared at it. It hopped after them through the trees as they made their way to the stage.

No, Lally's nervousness wasn't about the show. A plan was forming in her mind. It scared her silly every time she thought about it but one thing was sure: that puppet had to go. And the only one who could make that happen was her.

TWENTY-NINE

The first performance went beautifully.

The island had looked wonderful with its weeping willows and its lights. The weather was lovely, perfect for an outdoor show. The trip boats came all the way from Camden Town, their passengers happy and excited, already entertained by their trip along the canal. The barges lined up in a semi-circle as close to the island as they could moor. On the towpaths people gathered with deckchairs and folding stools and filled every space available. The giant screen had been rigged on a pontoon to one side of the island. The cameras were set up to film from two different angles and the camera guy was efficient and unobtrusive.

That first show on Friday night, it was as if someone had cast a magic spell and Lally had enjoyed it despite everything. The audience became hushed, entranced by the story, by the spectacle. As the haunting music spread out across the water an atmospheric mist rose off the pool. The island seemed enchanted, cocooned from the massive city.

Everyone had felt it. Lally couldn't tell how much it had to do with being visible, how much it had to do with the surroundings and how much was the play itself but she'd never had such an amazing experience as a performer. Throughout the play, she knew she needed to keep watching for an opportunity to do it – the thing she planned to do. But as that first show went by she was swept up in the magic of it.

Now it was Saturday; time for the matinee show. If she didn't act soon she might not get another chance. Another chance to get rid of that puppet.

She'd swear the horrid thing was watching her and somehow knew what she was thinking of doing. And whenever she looked up, the jackdaw was there in the trees, looking down.

Carla was in the audience, watching the show for the first time. Nette had decided she was well enough to come over from *Bird* on one of the trip boats. Lally wondered if Carla was enjoying it. She seemed to have forgotten all her anxiety about the hawthorn puppet now, now that she was getting better.

The interval was just over and Lally was working the swan girl. Eoin had the witch. They began the dance sequence. Eoin had redesigned it so that he and Lally were dancing with the puppets, moving around each other gracefully to the plaintive slow air of 'The Lonesome Boatman'.

Do i diddy, do i diddy dum dum!

The audience on the barges jumped and then laughed. A few people tutted. Some idiot had left their mobile phone on, someone with a really loud and ridiculous ring tone. It momentarily broke the spell and sent Lally slightly off course. She jerked her wrist and her swan tipped wings with the witch puppet. Lally drew back but not before she'd seen the tiny green flicker and felt an electrical jolt in the strings.

Eoin glanced at her quickly. She kept her eyes on her puppet and didn't acknowledge that she'd noticed anything. They continued the dance but the next time the puppets came close Lally dropped her hand down and touched the witch's strings.

This time everyone saw the green lights. They sparked and spun around the puppet, leaving the audience gasping and clapping at this unexpected special effect. Lally's fingers felt as if they had touched fire and she had to step backwards to keep her balance. Eoin was staring at her in alarm and seemed to be having trouble controlling the puppet. Lally met his eyes. She felt her anger and fear rush across her face, then turned away. She automatically glanced over to Carla. She was on her feet, her face chalk-white.

When the curtain fell Eoin didn't wait for encores. He took the witch puppet and went off stage. Nette stepped out in front of him.

'What in God's name was that?' she demanded.

He brushed past, almost knocking Nette over, jumped on board the *Beetle* and disappeared below. Nette hurried after him and as the puppeteers took another bow Lally could hear her banging on Eoin's cabin door.

'What was that, Eoin? What's going on?' Her voice was muffled.

Onstage, Claudine, Des, Lally and Gilles bowed again, their fingers causing their puppets to bow in front of them. They all heard the cabin door rattling and Nette shouting.

In her seat on the trip boat Carla was sitting still, the only person not clapping and cheering. She was staring at Lally, her good hand straying to the back of her neck where the splinter had been.

Another bow and the curtains came across. The barges began to leave and the puppeteers stepped offstage, stopping to hook their puppets onto the stand as they went, first Des, then Claudine, then Lally and Gilles. As she soon as she had her hands free Lally jammed her fingers into her mouth to cool them. Gilles pulled them back and held them to the light.

'My God, Lally,' he said, his eyes full of concern. 'They're burned!'

'Do you believe me now?' she asked. 'About the puppet?'

He nodded slowly. '*Oui*. There were green sparks,' he said. 'I saw them.'

'It felt like an electric shock,' Lally said. 'That's what Eoin thought happened to Carla to make her fall. A shock.'

'I saw Carla's face just now.' Gilles nodded. 'It was as if she understood ... recognised. And the mist, where is it coming from? This isn't normal weather for mist. What's going on?'

'I told you, it's that puppet,' Lally whispered, pulling him well out of earshot of the others. 'Every bad thing that's happened this summer has happened because of her. Eoin is sick. It's her fault. I - I don't think he'll ever be himself again as long as she's still here.'

Gilles looked at her fingers again. 'What do you want to do?' he said.

'I want to get rid of her, destroy her.'

'How do we do that? Eoin never lets her out of his sight.'

Lally frowned. 'I know. That's why it has to be done onstage, during a show. It has to be tonight. I'm not sure exactly how, but we have two hours before this evening's curtain up to work it out.'

19th June

I *am in hell.*

Whoever named this space beneath the stage for Satan's den named it well. It's dark and hot and I am suffering. Sweat's pouring from my brow and soaking my shirt. The heat of the theatre seems to burn here. Or perhaps it's my ravelled humours have me over-warm. Did I mention that I'm quaking like a celandine?

So far, all has gone to plan. At midday I tricked good Master Spragge into sending me on an errand. I arrived at the theatre two hours ago, well before the queues began outside. Hobbes met me backstage as prearranged and handed me a bag of old clothes and sheets.

'Has he done it?' I asked anxiously, taking the bundle in my arms. 'Has Bennet persuaded Master Waller to come to the play?'

'He has!' Hobbes said, opening the little door to hell and stuffing me in. 'He spun Master Waller a story of the audience calling out his name each night at the play's end. He said they want to behold him and applaud him to his face. Sure enough, the playwright's vanity was stroked.

Bennet could see that Master Waller was sorely tempted to attend but at the same tyme he kept casting anxious glances towards his work chamber – mind your head down there, Flea, you'll not be able to stand up full straight.'

'But how did Bennet persuade Master Waller in the end?' I asked.

'Ah! He is a clever baggage, is Bennet.' Hobbes grinned in at me, bent down double to look me in the eye. 'At first he pretends to regretfully accept Master Waller's protestations that he could not leave the house at present, see? Then he begins to walk away. Suddenly – and this is the stroke of genius – Bennet mentions how, some tyme back, he and me and Nashe brought a tree trunk to the house, intended for another play.

'"What a pity 'tis no longer here," he says to Waller, all innocence. "If only we had it now, it would fit in so beautifully with the third act."'

I have to admire Bennet. Such cunning! By seeming to think the trunk long gone he avoided rousing the playwright's suspicions, whyle simultaneously delivering the poor man a reason to bring the cursed thing to the theatre with him.

'And Waller, in his madness, seems to have forgot you and all the fuss you made about the abominable thing.' Hobbes chuckled. 'Bennet and Tom are to accompany him here just before the play begins. They'll bring the trunk in a wheelbarrow.'

And so our objective – to get both man and tree out of the house – has been realised.

Hobbes kept the door open to allow me some light till I'd made my way to just beneath the trapdoor.

'Till Act Four,' he whispered, and everything became dark.

There's quite a bit of stuff lying about down here, broken things and old props. I emptied the bag of cloths Hobbes gave me onto the earth directly under the trapdoor and sat myself upon them, listening, as the theatre door opened and the audience rushed in. The musty smell is making my nose twitch; I've had to smother several sneezes already. I jumped like a coney when the trumpet sounded!

The play is in its second act now. The boards above me have some gaps and chink-holes and if I screw my eyes up tight I can see the actors stride about and just about make out their features and their gestures. And I can see the heavens – the small canopy above the stage – a Coventry blue sky with clouds floating across it and angels' heads in each of the corners.

I can hear the lines of the play, though my heart is pounding and the actors' voices rise and fall a bit as they walk to and fro, upstage and down. I must follow things closely so as to know the tyme when I am to play my part.

Master Waller is here, sitting onstage above me, well off to the right. A squint through the boards tells me how ill and crazed he has become. He dribbles constantly and mouths the words of the play, ahead of tyme, every third word being said aloud. The hawthorne trunk is within his sight, part of the furniture of Frideswide's chamber. Later it will be dressed with a crown of willow branches and represent a tree in the forest where Frideswide and her maid are abandoned after their abduction. That scene is when my turn to act comes.

I will make the tree trunk disappear!

What if the sprite within the tree senses my fear and awakes? What if I cannot do what I promised to do? What if it all goes awry?

I tear my eyes away from the hawthorne. I concentrate on the voices. I'm all fret and tremble, awaiting my cue, crouching beneath the trapdoor, here in hell.

THIRTY

E oin didn't emerge from his cabin until the Saturday evening show was due to start. Again he refused to answer questions about what had happened at the matinee. He held the puppet close and walked past them all, off the *Beetle* onto the island to take his starting place onstage.

The first half went as usual. As soon as the interval came he shot offstage and disappeared into his cabin again. Everyone else stood around in the chow house drinking water.

'Carla said I was to look at your fingers, Lally,' Nette said. 'Are they all right?' Carla had come over with the trip boats again but this time she was on the island sitting alone on a deckchair hidden under one of the willows. 'I would have looked at them this afternoon but the trip boat guy said if I wanted a lift back to *Bird* with Carla I had to go right away.'

Lally nodded. 'They're fine. I'm fine.'

'What happened out there this afternoon, Lally?' Nette said. 'Where did—'

'It's time,' Gilles interrupted.

Des looked at his watch. 'We've another couple of minutes, I think.'

'Your watch must be slow.' Gilles showed Des his phone. 'See. We're late, actually.'

'Better get back up there, so.' Des got to his feet. Claudine and Nette were also looking at their watches but Gilles shooed them towards the stairs.

'*Vite, vite,* slowcoaches,' he said, waving his arms at them and laughing. 'We can't be late for the last act. Go, go!'

'Eoin,' Lally called over towards the closed cabin door. 'Eoin, we're going up. It's time.'

As soon as the words were out she moved quickly and quietly the short distance to the cabin door and Gilles crept after her. They could hear Eoin approaching the door as Gilles hid just around the corner on the stairs.

Lally held her breath at the sound of Eoin's key turning in the lock. She planted her feet firmly on the floor and waited for the door to open.

'Look at my fingers!' she shouted, sticking her left hand up into Eoin's face as soon as he appeared. 'Look what that thing did to me.'

He started back from her in surprise, staring at her upraised fingers, which made it easy for Lally to reach out and grab the witch puppet with her rubber-gloved right hand.

Please let the glove protect me, she thought. Please.

Before Eoin could react Gilles sprang out of his hiding place and headbutted him in the stomach. Eoin fell backwards, releasing his grip on the puppet. The last thing Lally saw as Gilles slammed the cabin door shut was the look of shock on her dad's face. There was a howl as he realised what they were doing but Gilles already had the door handle jammed shut with a sweeping brush.

Lally held the witch puppet as far away from her body as she could and wrapped a towel around her.

'Ready?' Gilles said.

Lally couldn't speak. She looked at the cabin door where the handle was rattling furiously against the broom.

'It's holding,' Gilles said. 'Come on, we have to get up onstage.'

Lally held out her left hand. Gilles produced another black rubber glove and pushed it onto her fingers, gave them a gentle squeeze, then turned her around, avoiding touching the puppet. 'Go, go!'

On the island they both ignored the curious glances of Des, Claudine and Nette. Gilles went straight to the puppet stand and unhooked the swan girl.

'What's Gilles doing?' Nette whispered. 'Lally? Where's Eoin? What in blazes is going on now?'

Lally didn't answer. She stepped behind the screen, drawing the towel off the witch puppet as she went. The music began to play, the mournful opening notes of 'The Lonesome Boatman' silencing the audience. Gilles stepped onstage and placed the swan girl on the waves, her head tilted sadly to one side. The curtain rose and mist swirled up from the pool as Lally entered with the witch, carefully unfurling her wings. She

238

could feel the thing come to life, small waves of energy running up the strings through the wooden control, pulsing against the rubber gloves.

Lally began the dance. But this dance would not be one of reconciliation and forgiveness, as Eoin had written it; this would be a dance of blame and anger, a dance to the death. Gilles and the swan girl registered shock, then began to tremble with fear.

Lally and the witch-of-the-air advanced on the swan child; the swan child struck out and retreated. The witch began to spark and fizz, and the audience reacted first with gasps, then with pantomime hissing. The swan girl counter-attacked and the audience cheered. The witch struck out, the swan dived beneath the waves. The witch skimmed the surface, searching, seeking; the swan child attacked from behind. The witch recoiled, and the swan child rose high above her, hovered for a moment, then dropped, beak first, towards the cowering witch. As she came, the witch began to glow, an unpleasant green fluorescent sheen. She snarled (or was it Lally who snarled? She couldn't tell) and flew upwards to meet the attack. Their wings met in a tangle of black and white.

Suddenly a tiny green flame sparked into life and the swan girl's feathers flared and sizzled. Gilles spun her away behind the screen stage right, gathered her into his body and patted the smouldering white wing with his hand. He held her protectively, looking out at Lally.

'Now,' he whispered. 'It has to be now.'

But Lally was already losing control of the puppet. The hawthorn witch was fighting her, sending ever stronger currents up the strings. The reinforced rubber pads of the gloves were softening, melting. She heard a scuffle from behind the screen.

'Here, take these.' Gilles was grabbing the puppets already hanging on the puppet stand and shoving them at Nette, Claudine and Des. They took them from him automatically, their mouths opening and closing in confusion. He rolled the stand out onto the stage and Lally stumbled towards it. She practically threw the puppet onto a hook and wrenched her hands away, pulling them from the melting gloves. She fell backwards, sprawling over the plywood waves that ran across the stage. There was a mixture of puzzled gasping and giggling from the audience. Gilles stepped forwards. He held up a can in his hand and everyone fell silent.

The witch's small black eyes glared at Gilles, her head upright, her wings spreading as if someone was still working her strings. He popped the lid on the can and pressed hard on the top, blasting out a cloud of sickly scented hairspray.

'The witch must die!' he shouted, throwing his arms out to the audience in a direct appeal.

'The witch must die!' repeated the audience on the barges, leaning forwards in their seats, their mouths all ohhs and ahhs of surprise.

'Die!' came the echoing shout from the crowd on

the towpath watching the action on the screen.

Lally pulled the London Bridge lighter from her leggings pocket and got back to her feet. A resounding crash from the *Beetle* startled her for only a second. Eoin must have bashed his cabin door open. He'd be out here soon, coming to save his creation. Lally wobbled, stepped forward and flicked the lighter into life.

Your element is fire, witch; that's what the stuff on the Internet said, Lally thought. Well, let's fight fire with fire.

She held the little flame towards the filmy black wings. 'The witch must die,' she yelled.

Act Four

'**M**i'lady, someone comes!'
There it is – the signal it's my tyme to act. I
unhook the latch on the trapdoor and ease it inwards. Tom
glances down at me and winks.

'At last, Frideswide, you are mine!' cries a voice from
above, and suddenly Bennet is flying down from the
heavens, swooshing across the stage on a rope, scooping
up Tom – Frideswide – as he passes.

They land lightly, well to stage right of the opening
to hell. Hobbes comes flying after them, thumping to
his feet very close to the trapdoor. All three together
are blocking Master Waller's view of the hawthorne
trunk, and Frideswide and her maid are squealing fit
to pierce your ears through besides. As Hobbes
straightens back up to his feet he deftly knocks the tree
trunk backwards through the trapdoor. I jump to one
side as it topples on to the soft bed of old curtains I
have arranged to muffle the sound of its fall here in
hell.

This is the moment I have been dreading. I have a

cloak in my hands with which to wrap it, but for now I am transfixed.

What if the sprite within awakes?

A sharp stamp from above makes me look up. Faire Frideswide is screaming for all she is worth and fighting off her attackers. All is chaos onstage but Hobbes is waving his hands downwards to remind me to shut the trapdoor. I push it back up into place and I am alone in the dark.

With it. With her.

Above my head the battle for Frideswide's honour has commenced; more shrieks, the clash of swords, bodies hitting the boards and rolling about.

I creep towards the hawthorne trunk, the cloak in my hands, as if I am attempting to trap a wild animal with a net. I flick my hand out quickly, and snatch away the willow crown that has adorned it onstage. I fling it behind me and wipe my fingers on my breeches as if they are unclean. I circle on tiptoe, delaying the moment I must touch the trunk itself.

'Woe is me, woe, woe, woooooooe!'

Frideswide's dying moan. Now silence will fall and the whole theatre will become still, as cast and audience realise she is about to breathe her last. I stop still too, and wait for the pitiful final scene.

'Waaaarrraagh!' A hideous wail comes from stage right. Master Waller! He has noticed that the trunk is gone. I glance upwards and see his form through the chinks; he's lurching towards the trapdoor.

That gets me moving, sharpish! I jump to, smothering

the trunk in the red cloak and rolling it over so it lies all within the velvet. I quickly tie two ends together to form a sling to keep the tree within and grab the other two corners in my hands. Above my head Master Waller is walloping the trap, screaming like a man possessed. The door bounces under his assault. I can hear the confusion of the audience. Bennet tries to speak his lines as if all is normal.

The hawthorne trunk is heavy. I can barely move it.

I cast one more look up at the trapdoor and to my horror I realise the latch is not full over. Each crash of Waller's fist is working it out of place. I hurl myself and my load to one side just as the latch undoes and the door slams inwards. For a second Master Waller is hanging over the side, huge eyes blinking down at me, then he is tumbling in.

He lands upside down, legs akimbo, arms splayed. One look in those wild eyes and I take to my heels! I drag the trunk after me through the darkness. It bumps and catches in some things and I bump and catch in others. I am bent down like an old hunchback, peeling my eyes for the way out. I can hear Master Waller scrambling to his feet behind me as I pitch myself from hell. I shove open the door to the backstage area with my shoulder, straighten up too soon and smash my forehead as I come out.

Ow! Ow! Ow!

I blink about in the gloom. Now what? In the original plan Hobbes was to meet me here and help me get the thing up the steps to the wheelbarrow, but he's still on stage, I can hear him speak his second to last line. No tyme to wait.

I thump frantically up the little flight of steps. How I drag the cursed hawthorne with me, I do not know – fear lends me strength, I suppose.

Where's the wheelbarrow? It's meant to be here, right here, waiting! Where is it? There! The stagekeeper's got it, up behind the curtain. He's taking it away.

'That's mine!' I hiss. 'Leave off it! I need it.'

He drops the handles in surprise at seeing me approach and I gather the cloak back around the tree trunk and make to heave it into the barrow. The effort is too much and I stumble as it goes in. I catch the edge of the hanging behind me, the tapestry which hides the backstage area from the view of the audience.

I hear a ripping and then a slooshing sound and the hanging comes rippling down in a cloud of dust. Light floods that dark space. There is a puzzled silence and then a great wave of laughter. Horrified, I turn slowly around.

Every eye in every head in that theatre is looking at me, every hand is pointing a finger. The actors have given up all pretence of the play now. I stare helplessly out at them and they stare back.

Suddenly Waller erupts from under the stage, exploding upwards at my feet. Somehow the willow crown has attached itself to his head, and a small painted bird is tangled in its branches. Various chains and silk flowers have hooked themselves about him. He looks like some crazed forest monarch emerging from the underworld. He stumbles up to me, reaching for her, the thing in the barrow.

She'll awake at his touch. I am certain she will, and then all will be lost.

I grab the handles and run the barrow onstage. He comes after me. We begin a lurching frantic circle, weaving amongst the actors. This delights the crowd, tickled to find the tragedy turned comic.

'Run, your highness,' someone yells. 'Run and you'll catch the knave!'

A thousand voices cheer Master Waller on as I duck around Tom and dive between Nashe and Hobbes and he follows, gibbering all the whyle. Hobbes steps forward then and grasps him around the waist, lifting him effortlessly into the air. The playwright kicks his legs helplessly, his arms still outstretched towards me.

'My lady!' he screeches. 'He steals her from me! He absconds with my love!'

The crowd look from him to me and at that moment the cloaked trunk in the barrow does indeed seem to be more woman than wood.

'I'll save her!' yells a groundling right at the front. He throws one leg onstage. 'I'll save yer lady for ye!'

Nashe steps forward and kicks the man back down into the pit. The crowd's laughter breaks on us like a thunderclap. Another man is hoisting himself onto the boards, stage left, and two more are being hoisted by their friends, stage right. Bennet and Nashe shove them back, but several more rush the stage from every side. One drunken idiot is making to drop down from the balcony above. Hobbes has his hands full with Master Waller who still cries and wriggles and reaches for me. I am trying to back away from him, but the baying crowd has me transfixed and my feet seem suddenly boneless, the stage all made of sand. Above our heads the crows burst into an agitated clamour.

'Flea!' a voice yells right in my ear. Someone pinches my arm urgently. Faire Frideswide tosses back her golden curls and glares at me.

'Run!' shouts Tom. 'Run for your life, Flea!'

THIRTY-ONE

Something erupted above Lally's head and shot out of the twilight like a small black rocket.

'Ka-aaak! Ka-aaak!' The jackdaw passed so close to her face one wing smacked her skin. She ducked.

The lighter went out. She flicked it. Damn! Was it empty? The bird had turned and was coming at her again. She could hear the audience gasping, hear the wings approaching.

Flick. Flick. Flick. A flame.

Now, she thought. I have to do it this time. The puppet was sending waves of energy towards her, pressing her back.

Lally forced her hand forwards, the tiny flame wobbling. Gilles had really soaked the puppet in hairspray. The slightest touch of the lighter should be enough.

'Ya-ah!' She threw herself sideways just as the bird returned, trying to fly between her and the puppet. She heard the flame hiss, saw a black wing catch fire – but whose wing, bird or witch? She smelled something burning through the lingering hairspray, then the jackdaw was coming again, cawing furiously. It was diving straight for her and there was nothing to do but to run. Stage left, under one of the willows. She tried to duck beneath a low branch and felt her forehead make sharp contact with wood. Suddenly she was falling off the island's edge into the dark water where the pretty lights weren't twinkling.

'Lally!' she heard Gilles shout as she went down.

Someone screamed. Was it her own voice? One way or other her mouth was full of water. It caught in her throat. She hadn't expected the pool to be so deep. She broke the surface for a second, long enough to spit up, snatch a brief breath and hear Nette cry, 'But, Des, you can't swim.' Then she was going down again.

Des can't swim? Lally thought. But I can. I can swim. Why can't I swim?

Something was catching at her legs. She kicked frantically but the more she struggled the tighter the thing coiled about her ankles. Her throat was constricting, fighting to cough and clear itself. One desperate upward surge and she broke the surface again and caught another jagged breath.

She briefly saw everyone on the island and heard them screaming her name. In the middle of them the witch puppet was hanging there on the wooden stand. Flames were beginning to eat her wings, hair and clothes, outlining her little wooden body against the night sky.

The strings. They were burning yet they were holding. They should be falling apart. The witch puppet should be falling apart.

As the water tugged her back down she saw Eoin come roaring onto the stage.

'Where is she? Where is she? What have you done with her? You'll not have her,' Lally heard him yell. 'She's mine! She's mine!'

Then the weeds tightened their grip on her legs and she sank down.

Now

*W*hat if she awakes? What havoc will she visit on me? I've made it out of the theatre and through the trees, towards the river.

Lion, Ram, Elephant. The Saracen's Head, the Crane, the Bull 'n' Swan. I tick off the names of the inns as I pass them, half-walking, half-running, steering the wheelbarrow with one hand and keeping the other atop the trunk to stop it toppling out.

I am petrified. In my mind's eye I see that face, the eyes, those talons descending. The cloak suddenly feels warm under my fingers and I'm thinking a pale green glow is pulsing through a threadbare patch in the velvet.

If she feeds on imagination then I must stop imagining, I tell myself frantically. Think of something ordinary.

Home. My mother baking bread.

No, that won't do, for now I'm imagining the smell in the air and the taste on my tongue.

Right turn. This lane is half empty. Thank God, thank God.

Lessons at old Master Hinke's school. Learning to

251

form my letters: a, a, a, a, A, A, A, A over and over and over...

The alarming green light dims as I turn another corner, around by the cathedral. This street is full of people and carts and I seem to be going entirely against the tide. A dog begins to chase me, snarling and snapping at my heels. I aim a kick at it but then I realise it's making me go faster and let it be. Soon I'll be at the bridge. A, A, A, B, B, B.

'Flea!'

I turn my head. Bennet! He's just rounding St Mary Overy's. Thank goodness. Someone to share this load. I stop to wait for him, lower the wheelbarrow slightly, and the hound pounces. But it's the hawthorne he goes for. He sinks his teeth into a piece of exposed wood and sets to worrying it. This only lasts a second. He leaps away with a pained yelp. Down go his ears and his long tail. He casts me an astonished look and scarpers away.

Bennet is still a way off, waving his hands frantically at me. 'Run, Flea, run,' he shouts.

There's Hobbes behind him in the narrow lane. He halts too, plants his feet firmly, spreads his great arms on either side and braces himself in the entrance to the street. I quickly see why. A dozen heads – no, a score, two score – appear behind him.

The groundlings! They're out of the playhouse and giving chase.

Bennet is close now, but I do not dare wait for him to reach me.

'B, B, B, B,' I chant, lifting the wheelbarrow and breaking

into a ragged run. 'C, C, C, C, D!'

A twist, a turn, the bridge-gate, squash through all them that's coming and all them that's going, sorry, sorry, beg pardon, mind your toes, mind how you goes, D, D, D, E. Hurry, hurry, Bennet, hurry. Stitch in my side. Double up. Ow, ow, sorry, sorry, mind your toes.

'Flea!' Bennet's voice behind me, getting closer. 'Hobbes couldn't hold them, Flea, they're nearly on us. Run, Flea!'

But the crowd before me on the bridge is so dense and the way between the houses and shops so narrow.

'FLEAS!' I shout suddenly. 'A PLAGUE OF FLEAS! LET ME THROUGH OR CATCH MY ITCH!'

It works. Startled faces back away and the crowd splits in front of me. I dash through, looking for one of the few gaps between the buildings where the bridge wall can be accessed and I can see the water.

There, there.

'FLEAS!' I shout again and turn towards it.

Smash, crash. The trunk snags on the legs of a stall and a thousand tiny pins tinkle to the ground. The pin-seller starts to scream shrilly; I ignore her and almost run the wheelbarrow into the wall. I lower it and try to haul the trunk out onto the balustrade. But it's so heavy I can't do it. I can't.

Try, try! There's the water, down below, hurtling out between the pillars of the bridge. One big heave and she'll be gone.

And she's awakening at last, now that I have my arms

about her. The load within the cloak is twitching and writhing like a weasel and I want to drop it. Drop it and run away, run away home all the way to Chiswick. Tears are blinding my eyes.

I mustn't fail now. Heave, heave!

But try as I might, I cannot lift the cursed thing on my own.

'Flea! Quick, Flea!' Bennet breaks through the crowd, and right behind him the groundlings come charging.

'Stop him,' their leader yells. 'That's a woman he's got!'

'He's going to throw her into the river!' screeches an old dame.

'She's already dead, I'd say,' shouts another.

'No, see? She moves!'

'Get him!' they shout together. 'Grab him.'

'Stay back!' Bennet's voice rises above them and brings them to a halt. His command is all that's between me and the baying rabble. That, and the pin-seller. She has grabbed a pole and is swinging it at the crowd to keep them off her precious merchandise.

My stomach has turned to water now. Those people look fit to tear me limb from limb and the thing in my arms is awake. I swallow hard.

'Do not frighten him,' Bennet urges the crowd. 'Let me talk him away from the edge.'

His expression seems to seek their approval and they consent. All eyes on me and him. Over his shoulder I see a wild figure fighting through the crowd – Master Waller in his forest crown. He opens his mouth to accuse me but two large hands come from behind him, wrapping about his waist and covering his mouth. Hobbes!

'Here, boy,' Bennet says to me in a pleading tone. 'Do not do anything desperate now. Everything will be all right, just hand her over to me and all will be well.'

He reaches out his hands as if to take the hawthorne from me and only I see his wink. I slump and lower my end as if I give in. Quick as a trace he leans down and grabs the other end from mine. One, two, and together we heave it over the wall.

As I feared, the sprite is full awake. The cloak spins away from the trunk as we swing it out from the balustrade and let go. She emerges as the hawthorne starts to fall. Her arms unfold, those long hands flash out. But she must go where her host tree goes. She snarls and reaches up; those evil fingers catch one of my forearms and one of Bennet's too. As we both snatch our arms back, her nails drag through our skin, raking deep lines, but finding no purchase. She tumbles downwards, down down into the raging water, her black eyes widening in surprise. Suddenly the air above us cracks into a jagged cacophony of caws. Bennet and I duck as the crows swoop low over us and spread out over the river.

We straighten up. We've done it, she's gone.

THIRTY-TWO

Stay calm, Lally screamed inside her head. Don't open your mouth! Don't open your mouth!

But even as she thought it her lungs demanded air and her mouth tried to deliver. Water rushed in, up her nose, down her throat. She could see nothing now but blackness.

'Where is she?' Was that Eoin shouting, somewhere above her? 'Where's Lally?'

Something hit the water nearby with a bang. The pool shifted all about her but she was passing out. Her legs were still twitching against the rope-like weeds and her arms were still reaching above her, but her head was exploding. Part of her brain was drifting away, shutting it all out, shutting it all down.

Don't give up, Lally McBride. Don't close your eyes,

But she couldn't keep them open; she wasn't even sure she was inside her body any more, except for something tugging urgently on her wrist. Then she was being dragged upwards, wrenched free of the water weeds. She was back at the surface, coughing and gulping, and a familiar hand was holding her chin.

'Breathe, Lal. Please breathe, love,' Eoin's voice said right at her ear. 'I have you. I have you. You're safe.'

When the fighting for breath had stopped, when she'd spat out half the pool and her throat was functioning normally again, Lally looked at the stage. The witch puppet was ablaze. As she watched, the strings finally began to disintegrate.

They shouldn't have held this long, Lally thought again. They should have been the first things to burn. But they were giving way at last, despite the puppet. In a moment she would be in pieces on the boards. What if she set fire to the curtains as she fell? The puppet stand was ablaze already. Would the whole stage go up? The old willow trees too?

Someone darted out from under the trees – Carla.

'Stay clear,' she yelled as she kicked the stand towards the water. It careened sideways, bumped against the stage edge, and toppled slowly off. As it fell the witch puppet broke away from it. She swung out over the water, her burning limbs disconnecting in mid-air as the leather joints burnt through.

'She's mine, you won't hurt her,' Lally heard Eoin whisper. 'She's mine,' he repeated, pulling Lally in tight to him and putting his body between her and the thing flying from the stage.

Some pieces landed a little close; an upper arm, a palm, some fingers. Eoin tensed and batted them away but Lally could see they were charred through. They hissed as they bobbed on the surface of the pool. For a few seconds the smoke smelled strange, fetid, rank, rotten, and then it was gone.

257

The audience on the trip boats were on their feet. They'd been transfixed by the unexpected pyrotechnics and unsure whether the puppeteers' antics in the water were real-life drama or part of the show. The camera guy looked baffled and uncertain what to do next. The audience on the towpath had only seen what the screen had shown them – the burning puppet. Someone on the nearest boat began to clap and eventually everyone else joined in.

'Are you OK?' Gilles was in the water, a life buoy in his hands.

'We're fine,' Eoin said. 'Bring that buoy over to Nette so she can get Des in. They look like they're struggling a bit there.'

Lally looked around her. Had everyone jumped in the water after her? Pretty much. Nette was hanging on to Des a few metres over to her right. Claudine was treading water close by. Only Carla was still on the island, standing at the water's edge, staring warily at what remained of the charred wood.

Gilles swam towards Nette and Des despite their protests.

'First time I've ever seen Des take a ducking,' Eoin chuckled. 'Believe me, I'll not be letting you live this down in a hurry, Dessie O'Neill. Come on, let's get everyone back on dry land.'

'You're all right,' Gilles whispered. They were on the *Beetle*, sitting on the roof, wrapped in towels and blankets, hot chocolates in hand. The audience had dispersed at last, the stage and lighting people had gone. 'Everything's all right now, yes?'

Lally nodded.

He squeezed her hand and got up to help his mother bring a tray of sandwiches from the galley.

Lally looked around her. Someone had forgotten to turn off the twinkly lights on Browning's Island and it all looked a little dishevelled now the stage was empty. Still, with the stars and the weeping willows and the lights and the hot chocolates, everything felt good.

Yes, everything was all right.

She would ask her questions some time, some time soon, but the answers didn't matter so much now. All the anxiety of the last few weeks was falling away from her, that awful feeling of threat in the air was gone. She was suddenly sure that she would go to Paris with Gilles and Claudine after all. She'd find a way to make it happen. And she'd have a future with college and stuff away from the barge. But the *Beetle* would always be home and Nette, there, picking green gunge out of her hair, and Carla, there, smiling for the first time in weeks – they would always be her mums.

Eoin, sitting beside her, close beside her, was himself again too. She could see it in his eyes. Blue eyes that looked very like her eyes. She'd never noticed that before.

Was he her father? Maybe he was. Maybe he wasn't.

Maybe she'd never know for sure. But at this moment, she knew exactly who he was.

'Dad,' she said.

He grinned at her and reached his hand out to tousle her hair. Lally threw her arms around him and buried her head in his shoulder.

'Dad.'

The last of it

'*U*uuuuuuuh!' *A hundred breaths all sucked inwards at the same tyme warn Bennet and me that the danger is now at our backs. We both turn around.*

Bennet laughs. A big, hearty laugh.

I do not think that is a good idea, but it does cause the crowd to hesitate. And the pin-seller, bless her, is still swinging her pole.

'Fine folk!' Bennet says cheerily. (Isn't he afraid? How can he not be afraid?) 'Our play is at an end!' he announces, as he puts his injured arm to my back. He drops a bow and pushes me forward into one too.

The expressions on the faces in front of us are wavering as we straighten up. They settle into angry confusion.

Bennet points over the wall and invites someone to come and look. The pin-seller nods her reluctant consent and two men move forwards.

The hawthorne has travelled quite a distance in the quick water but some accompanying crows still mark its position.

'Tis only a bleedin' log!' one man reports, in a slightly disappointed tone.

Nashe and Tom come, pushing their way to the front of the crowd. They step delicately over the barricade of pins, warily eyeing the pin-seller and her weapon. They face our audience with us. Tom stands at my left. Bennet is at my right. Nashe at his right. Hobbes still has Master Waller in his arms. The man seems to be gasping for breath and is flailing his arms about as if he is in the water with her who infected him. Hobbes takes the crazy crown of branches off our master's head and holds him in a gentle bear hug.

Bennet smiles at the groundlings again, that smile I used to fear.

'We actors tread the boards in play,' he says, calm as you like.

'Today we took our play away.

'Into the streets we led you hence (he waves his arms about, taking in the whole city)

'To give us chase, to join our dance.

'You – actors though you knew it not –

'Have played your parts full well,

'Twixt trick and twist, Faire Frideswide's tale

'You've joined with us to tell.'

He takes my right hand in his. To my surprise his hand is shaking as much as mine. He tightens his grip and our hands are still and strong.

'The Master of the Revels will have our hides for this,' he whispers. 'We may have to go tour the small towns for a few months to stay out of his way. We'll need someone

262

to do the work of stagekeeper and book-keeper. '

Me? He means me to join the company? And travel about as one of *Waller's Men?*

Tom takes my left hand. We four step forward, smiling brightly. We bow low. The crowd applaud.

'Now, we ask your leave to take our leave,

'Bid you farewell, our play is done!'

I glance quickly at the river below us. The hawthorne trunk has disappeared.

Our play is done.

ACKNOWLEDGEMENTS

My cousin, Sarah Fitzpatrick, joined the Puppet Theatre Barge in London several years ago and trained to be a puppeteer. Her emails telling me of her adventures working with and making puppets sparked the idea for this book. Thank you, Sarah! For sparking the idea, for the guided tours, the answers to all my questions; for reading early drafts and giving me detailed responses, and for your help and patience. I couldn't have done it without you!

You can go and see Sarah's beautiful puppets at www.missfitzmarionettes.com

The Puppet Theatre Barge is a real barge and a real theatre. It was set up in 1982 by Gren Middleton and Juliet Rogers, and it is with their kind permission I have used it as a setting for the modern story.

I have changed things. The real barge is called the *Maybrent*. I have turned her head on tail (her bows are where the *Beetle*'s stern is) and I have peopled her with characters and puppets of my own creation. Though there is a wonderful bear puppet, and also a rabbit, horse and zebra who live on one wall of the *Maybrent*, none of the characters in this book are based in any way on the real folk of the Puppet Barge.

The *Maybrent* spends the winter season moored in Little Venice and the summer season on the Thames at Richmond (I have switched the seasons in the book). It is a wonderful theatre space with gorgeous puppets and fantastic shows which have been entertaining and enthralling audiences for thirty years.

Thank you to Gren, Juliet, Kate, Rob and all the puppeteers of the Movingstage Marionette Company, for allowing me to attend rehearsals and for answering my endless questions. I hope it isn't too disconcerting to read this story woven around your reality!

Visit the Puppet Theatre Barge here: www.puppetbarge.com

The Children of Lir is an Irish legend. I have based my ideas of how it would work as a marionette piece on the beautiful Siamsa Tire dance version: www.siamsatire.com

For the Tudor story I visited the New Globe Theatre and got lots of help from the guides, especially Emmeline. Many thanks: www.shakespearesglobe.com

The guide at the Rose Theatre (56 Park Street, London, SE1 9AS) was really helpful too. If you would like to go to see the excavations or a play at the Rose check out the website: www.rosetheatre.org.uk

The Rose is open every Saturday from 10.00 a.m. to 5.00 p.m. Entry is free but donations are welcome!

Thanks to another helpful cousin, Mick Fitz, and his partner, Agnes, for correcting some French details, to Anna McCabe for help with medical details, to Adele Griffin for providing her Wexford haven as an emergency writing bolthole, and to Oliver Flood for loaning me his middle name!

As always, thanks to my editor Jenny Glencross and my husband Michael for making me work just that little bit harder and noticing the stuff I miss.

Marie-Louise